WITNESS THE NIGHT

Mallika Ahluwalia

Kishwar Desai has worked in print and broadcast media as journalist, scriptwriter, TV anchor, producer and the head of a TV channel in India. Her first book, *Darlingji: The True Love Story of Nargis and Sunil Dutt*, was published by HarperCollins *Publishers* India in 2007.

Kishwar lives between London, Delhi and Goa. This is her first novel; it was longlisted for the Man Asian Literary Prize, 2009.

Kishwar Desai

WITNESS THE NIGHT

HarperCollins *Publishers* India
a joint venture with

New Delhi

For Meghnad,
for dreaming up a wonderful life together

ONE

9/9/07

You asked me to write my thoughts. But there are too many questions in my mind, too many fears. First I would have to remove all those worries, only then can I think again. You cannot understand how painful it is. No one can.

How does one avoid the tyranny of dreams? The footsteps that keep taking you back to a house full of ghosts, where every window has a face staring from it, each face once beloved and known, now with bloodied eyes and grey lips, their hands drooping, bodies limp, yet yearning. They are all silent. The thick bile of sadness oozing from their hearts has regurgitated into their throats and blocked their voices, their pale shadowy hair seems like seaweed, green and stringy, floating in the air. Yet, all around their collapsed bodies is the scarlet odour of fresh killing, the meat at their feet is newly shredded for the dogs, which are peculiar and never bark. They do not even nudge the meat. Do they know whose flesh it is? How can they tell? Does human flesh taste different? Is there some loyalty hidden in the DNA of animals that allows them to differentiate? Nothing in the house is as it should be, because now another smell permeates and rises, the smell of burning flesh. The house is a shamshan ghat, and the phool have yet to be gathered... the flowers, because that is what bones are called when they are incinerated, they turn into white flowers.

Each of those faces at the windows, caressed by my hands and kissed by my lips, will be now poured, all white flowers, into earthen urns and drowned in the Ganga. The bubbles of dense unforgiving water will rise and grab each urn with greedy fingers, snap it away, yank it from my helpless hands. I will say thirteen prayers for each one of them, thirteen times mumble what I have been told to say.

The house, as I gaze upon it, sways in the wind.

It is raining, I love the rain. I stand perfectly still in the garden, in the tightening embrace of the night, and let the rain beat into my skin. I want to let it touch me all over, let my tears mingle with the steady downpour until I cannot tell the difference between my tears and the rain, till everything is within me, the rain, the clouds, the wind, and I am struck by each of those thousands of droplets into numbness, and my eyes are blinded as they are raised to the open sky, so I can no longer see the house, or the relentlessly loving faces in the windows. If I could escape I would, but where can I go?

I turn to run out onto the open road, take a rickshaw, get to the train station and leave for Delhi, as I have been told to do. But something holds me back. Is it the blood congealing on the white marble steps? I turn around again and, shivering in the cold rain, try to scrub my footprints in the rain water but the blood still pours out of the house, and the footprints form again, perfect and recognizable. I pull myself away because I slowly realize that the dark house, looming large out of the ground, is eternal, as though it was built along with the rest of the earth, for ever and ever. And looking out from each window, which I have left open so that the smell of burning flesh and bone can evaporate, will still stare all those vacant gentle faces, all thirteen of them, beckoning with listless eyes, their open fingers clasped in the sure grip of death.

But I did. I did run from there. Not very far, though. I only had to cross the road, and he was waiting for me. I was still crying and I kept wiping the blood from my hands. He had said we were going to Delhi to start a new life. But, standing there under an umbrella, he said we could not go immediately because we needed money. So he told me what to do. I was to go back to the house and when they found me, I should cry, just as I was doing now, and say that I had been unwell and asleep in my room. I had been woken up by the smell of burning flesh and as I came out of my room, I saw all these bodies, one after the other. I had become hysterical and was screaming and then someone assaulted me. I did not see the man, he was dressed in black, and he wore a mask. The servants were all on leave. I did not know what to do. I was feeling dizzy, and though I screamed for help, no one heard me because it was raining and it was so late at night.

We went back into the house then, the two of us, and he slapped me across my face because I was crying too much, and then he tied my hands and told me to struggle to release them so that marks would remain on my arms. It should look like someone had tried to hurt me, and tied me up. Even though we were surrounded by blood and burnt flesh, he pushed up my shirt and squeezed my breasts, and then he took me to my room, where he removed my salwar and pushed me down on the bed. I was feeling sick and did not want to do what he asked me to do, but he said he had to do this to me so our story seemed more credible. I listened to that familiar reasonable voice and drowned myself in the feel of his hands and his mouth.

ৡ

My eyes snap open and I stare at the ceiling. I look at the clock—3 a.m. The occasional flash of a passing car lights up the room. It is quiet, as only Jullundur can be quiet. After all those years of terrorism, when bomb blasts used to light up the night, now it is only car headlights. I reach for a cigarette. The pleasures of not sharing a room are many. You can fart in bed and you can smoke without asking, 'May I?' I look across the chintz printed bed sheets and imagine The Last Boyfriend sprawled there. Hairy, fat, rich. Better than bald, thin and poor. But unbearably attached to his 'Mummyji'.

Funny thing, this umbilical cord. If you're female, they can't wait to snip it off. But for boys, Mummyji's breasts drip milk like honey dew. I watched Boyfriend squirm with delight under Mummyji's gaze, as he piled on his millions in stocks and shares. With the ever increasing millions, and the solitaires glittering ever so brightly, why would Mummyji want a daughter-in-law dark and khadi-clad like me? I gently exhaled and blew Boyfriend away.

I can still hear Mummyji's shocked voice, the solitaires shaking in opprobrium: 'Simran, you are a sardarni, a Sikhni, and you smoke!'

I settle down on the bed more comfortably, lolling over the side where Boyfriend would have lain. The Punjab police guesthouse room smells of smoke. They say that once smoke enters the air-conditioning ducts, it keeps circulating there for years. Just like my Obsessive Compulsive Disorder, of not being able to erase a single detail from my mind.

Playing it over and over again. Like smoke it filters through my mind. The girl. The remand home. The theory I have, which is both a hypothesis and a nightmare. The scenario I have examined over and over again in my mind for three months. The only part that makes me uneasy is my inability to put the pieces together. Was there a man, an outsider? The girl denies it—but she had obviously been raped. Or was it murder in self-defence? Did she kill anyone? Did her brother or her father try to molest her? When they found her, she was covered with so many wounds and so much blood—her own as well as that of perhaps thirteen other people—that it was difficult to find out what had happened. And then, she could hardly speak. She was in hospital for three months and has just been shifted to a room near the jail, in judicial custody.

It worries me. Something tells me instinctively that the evidence is too obvious. From experience I know we have to redefine the boundaries—push away the walls that block us. As a professional but unsalaried social worker, rudely called an NGO-wali (and a rather amateur psychotherapist), I am shocked to find this poor traumatized fourteen-year-old orphan. In the last twenty-five miserable years I haven't seen a more sorrowful sight. I look through my notes, reading how every single member of her family had been poisoned and some of the victims stabbed with a knife. Since there was no other evidence or fingerprints, she is the chief suspect and under investigation. Once the police have finalized their case, she could, of course, be under trial for years as few cases in India ever come to the courts before at least twenty years. By that time she would be thirty-four years old and would probably be immune to any sort of reform and, if she isn't already, a murderess as well.

I light another cigarette. Shit, the electricity has just gone off. Why does anyone bother to live in this corrupt country? They screw you if you don't pay your taxes, but you can't do anything to them once you elect the damn ministers who live in palatial electric splendour while the rest of us scrounge around for a scrap of light. In full technicolour memory is a recent wedding: my mother's best friend's daughter married the son of a Minister in the Central Cabinet with Independent Charge. The wedding venue was lit up as though to guide a NASA spaceship to earth. The twenty lakh rupees spent on hiring generators for the various hotels and houses could have kept several hundred ordinary homes blazing with lights for a few years at least. My mother was moved to tears, of happiness of course, that her friend's daughter was being given away in a blaze of glory. She always said that if you have it, flaunt it. It was a long-standing tradition in her Punjabi family.

I fumble around and find a candle, then go back through my notes about the 'case' as I still think of it. Sweat trickles down my back. It is obvious that no one actually cared about Durga. Were it not for her large inheritance, the 'case' may not even have attracted the kind of publicity that it had. Perhaps the publicity would force an early decision?

I know what makes me uncomfortable—the danger of accepting the more obvious and easy explanations. I know, to my constant regret, that we sometimes take those options.

We could be tired and exhausted, the so-called criminal might not co-operate, the victim's family could be much more rigorous and demanding. Or influential and demanding. Yes, the justice system has been known to give up, and the wrong person ends up being convicted. If there is a conviction at all.

But of course, these days high-profile cases call forth candlelight vigils and activist journalism. Not that it helps, because thanks to mass vigilantism the courts are being pressurized into taking popular decisions. Democracy drives everything, you can even vote to hang someone today.

Just as well that, long ago, I veered away from becoming a lawyer. I chose the much more thorny but independent route of trying to help those who fall by the wayside. I know that sounds quite self-serving but let me tell you, smugness is the greatest attribute of the social worker in India, especially those like me who prefer to work as freelancers, at the non-government end of things. Because then I have the right to shout abuse at the mindless public machinery while virtuously continuing with my own prim attempt to improve things. Luckily, because the government has little thought or time for social welfare, I can wear my halo of righteousness with panache. My faultless tribe stands for the human rights of the downtrodden, the voiceless, faceless, nameless, and often blameless millions. So can't a little congratulatory self-promotion be forgiven amidst the hand-wringing and sobbing from the wings?

Of course, it may be an entirely mistaken notion that I have helped anyone at all. But it keeps me going till I occasionally reach the last bloody hole and drag out someone who has been kicked into the ground. Why do I do it? Sheer cussedness. Or, as my mother put it, I deliberately chose a profession that would make most bachelors (unless they were criminals or deviants) blanch. And scoot.

I prefer to do things the difficult way. When I think there has been a miscarriage of justice, I get into the system, meet everyone, represent no one, and try and get to the truth. I never know whether my efforts will be successful. Sometimes, someone will confess, or drop a hint. Funnily enough, the criminal community often trusts me because I am such an oddity, with my convent-school Hindi and salon-cut curly hair. I look so far removed from the world of shady deals and drugs and knives and punishment that they know I can't be a money-making lawyer or a fixer: I am just a powerless social worker, from my outsized red bindi to my kolhapuri chappals. When I tell them I want to see them free and living in a just world, they know I mean what I say because I wear my idealism like a brahmastra, ready to slay all the rakshasas.

Sometimes, they too begin to believe, like me, that there could be redemption (the convent school I went to taught me optimistic things about guilt, confession, redemption).

Actually, I have seen too many cases of criminals being 'reformed' and then going back to their old haunts and sinking into that familiar cycle of home-jail-home, until reality is completely distorted. In many cases it is difficult to distinguish the criminal from his circumstances, and then you understand that life can really be unfair. Now that they have discovered an infidelity gene, I suppose it is only a matter of time before they discover the 'criminal gene', and then what do we do? Open large gene reconstruction centres and get rid of jails? Or, after multiple experiments on mice, scientists will conclude that by injecting more serotonin and extracting testosterone, they can rectify the faulty chemical imbalance and we will become gentler, kinder, compassionate...

I thought I would never do this again (my last experience as a do-gooder had almost convinced me that there was no point to it), but when I read about this case, it intrigued me because it was in my home town, Jullundur. I had a very good idea what it was like to grow up as a small-town girl. It may sound like misguided conceit, but I thought I could understand Durga better than most people. I could perhaps help her cope with her distress. These days everything becomes 'a cry for help'. Killing thirteen people could also qualify for this, I suppose.

We all have our little weaknesses. Mine has always been to wade in where others feel it wiser not to. When Amarjit, an old college friend (we had shared our moments) who had always encouraged my work in the jails, and who was now Inspector General in Punjab, called me, I could not refuse. He wanted me to meet the girl, give her some support, help the police reach some sort of a decision, whatever it might be, about her mental health. He also felt responsible, because the girl's parents had been close friends of his. Now she had no one, except a sister-in-law in Southall, who had escaped death only because she had recently gone back to the UK. Her husband, Durga's brother, was dead.

So here I am, at 3 a.m., staring at a candle in a police guesthouse. My night clothes are full of sweat. I strip off and step under the shower, instantly relieved by the cool water. I randomly pick up each flabby forty-five-year-old breast and check it for lumps or bumps. Nothing. But I can't stop worrying. Are we somehow trapping a fourteen-year-old in a swamp of guilt? Could she have really killed thirteen people? In one night? All of them had been poisoned, some were slashed with a knife, a few had been half-heartedly burnt. Had it not been raining, it is possible that the house would have burnt down.

And she had been raped. Or had she? Is my judgement going haywire or am I being lured into the kind of pop psychology which brands female adolescent sexuality a crime? The Lolita syndrome. I am reminded uncomfortably of another case I read about, earlier today, which has probably affected me more than I thought. While the internet has shrunk the world, it has also made it bloodier, and less trustworthy. If in the past I had treated every case as unique, I know now I can always find something if not more gory than the one I am dealing with, then at least something which could provide a glimmer of understanding. If people grope the internet for soulmates, I click on to find twisted minds and tortured lives. And hopefully, some information about why they became the way they are.

This latest concerned a young girl called Billie Jo who had been killed in Hastings, in the UK. Her stepfather was accused of killing her. A teenager, she was stabbed to death while she was painting the front door. Some of the testimony seemed to imply that the adopted girl knew she was attractive, and used that to manipulate the father (who was a schoolmaster) and the other male teachers in her school. There was a suggestion of an illicit affair, of the stepfather not being able to control his own anger or his passion, or perhaps being blackmailed by his daughter. Ultimately he was acquitted. Clearly, the easy explanation isn't always the right one.

It is precisely the easy explanation I have to watch out for. As my mind sifts through various possibilities, I know that Durga's case fascinates me. The name itself is so apt—Durga, the fiery, many-armed goddess whose capacity for blood and mayhem is pure mythological theatre. However, the Durga I have come to examine in Jullundur's overcrowded jail seems terribly insecure and rather vacuous. We had our first meeting yesterday and I found myself at a complete loss.

Obviously, there is a chasm between us. I left Jullundur, a dusty, haphazardly constructed city in Punjab which resembles an ambitious village, when I was twenty. I broke all the rules and my mother's heart, as well as my engagement to a sardar who appeared to have a Very Promising Career in Hosiery. Initially, because all around me girls were being 'arranged' into marriages, I assumed that I had no choice, even though I was eighteen and above the age of consent. Fortunately, the lingerie business can be very liberating. Once I thought I had learnt enough about v-fronts and padded bras, and the difference between synthetic and natural fibres (mostly taught to me on long drives on a Vespa scooter which eventually meandered into fields of suitably long-stemmed sugarcane), I felt I should move on.

Now, returning to the same city, still unmarried but a woman of the world, veteran of several love affairs, seasoned traveller, an expert on 'Women in Incarceration: What Unfreedom Does to Women', twenty-five years later, what can I possibly have in common with a young, frightened girl who has been brought up in this provincial town?

Durga looks older than her years. I had seen pictures of her on TV but she is much thinner in real life. The snub nose and sulky full-lipped mouth are set in an oval face. When she was brought into the anteroom, on one side of the warden's office (I had insisted that I needed privacy), she was wearing a plain blue salwar kameez, not the jail uniform—a special concession, given that every high official in the government had known her parents, and known her since she was a child. It is embarrassing for them now to see her in the lock-up. And worse, she is still little more than a child. So a few allowances have been made for her: better food, proper clothes, occasional access to television. (Though I was told that it had been cut down after she reacted very badly to some of the coverage of the murders). By another court sanction the police have been able to seal off a room and keep her there.

None of these concessions would have made her popular with the other inmates. Fortunately, she does not have to see them. The sad thing is that she should not be here anyway. She should be in a proper juvenile home. Unfortunately, the juvenile home was recently raided and newspaper headlines screamed that many of the children were being sexually exploited and used for prostitution. So Durga has been put here, in a makeshift 'remand home for children'.

The regular Nari Niketan (the reformist institution for 'fallen' women) was another possibility, but it was also ruled out because of the high risk of exposure to drug and prostitution rackets. Or so I was told. In my experience, any institution which robs you of your freedom is a place where every kind of vice can be found, but if the courts have decided that she should be kept here, I cannot question it. Besides, till she agrees to see a lawyer, nothing can be done anyway. Right now, she is still too vulnerable and traumatized to be forced into any kind of situation.

Durga is not pretty, but she has a healthy, pink complexion

like most Punjabi girls from semi-rural India, who have been brought up on fresh milk and home-grown food. Yet she hunches as she sits down, anxious not to be noticed. Or at least, not have any attention drawn to her. Her clothes are loose and, even though she is tall and well built, she gives an impression of frailty, further enhanced by her meek demeanour.

I introduced myself.

She looked at me and looked away as though what she saw did not quite please her. I asked her to tell me about herself.

'I'm in Class 10, in St Mary's convent school.' She lapsed into silence and I could see tiny beads of sweat on her upper lip. She said nothing about her family; perhaps the thought of them was far too distressing.

'What subjects?'

'Literature, history... computers.' She was almost whispering now. Her English was accentless, which was also an indicator that her parents had belonged to the Punjabi upper-middle class, where the language is spoken clearly, and with few give-away inflections of the region.

'Durga...' I reached out to touch her hand lightly and she flinched as though I had hit her. On her arm I noticed a small, intriguing tattoo but she quickly covered it with her dupatta. For the first time, I noticed a light in her eyes. She seemed to smile. Or it may have been a nervous tic at the corner of her mouth.

'I'm here to help you, Durga. I'll come every day, and we'll talk about whatever suits you. Is there anything you want?'

'How long do I have to stay in here?' she asked softly, gazing at the dusty floor.

'I don't have the answer to that, but let's hope it won't be too long. Is there anything you want to talk to me about?'

She hung her head and said nothing. After that she completely withdrew and stared at the floor, as though there was a meaning in the squares of cement that puzzled her. I gave her some paper and asked her to write down anything she might want to share with me, and touching her briefly on the head, left.

So young! The thought drummed through my mind. It never failed to shock me. Over the years I had met children capable of the most vicious crimes and it always saddened me, the loss of a childhood. Very occasionally, they were freed and able to walk out, but usually they grew up behind bars, and despite all my attempts to educate them, get them into yoga, teach them music and song, even theatre, most of them I knew were just waiting for a chance to avenge themselves on the world that had robbed them of the one thing they would never enjoy again, their childhood.

I needed to get away from the claustrophobia of the city and the jail. I desperately needed a glass of cold beer. But I knew that in Jullundur a woman drinking in public would be an aberration. Indeed, during the days of terrorism, women here had been forced to cover their heads and threatened out of their jeans to wear only salwar kameez. No better than the Taliban.

Now, lying in bed in the stuffy guesthouse, early in the morning, I can still hear her voice, muffled by grief, perhaps even an inability to grasp the cards that life has dealt her. I can only hope that things will improve over the next few weeks. For the first time in my life, I doubt my ability to deal with a situation. Does she remind me of myself at fourteen?

Confused and depressed? Could I have ever killed another person?

I stub out the cigarette and try to sleep. The important thing is to remember to organize some liquor if I am going to stay on here. Should have brought some in my suitcase from Delhi.

To simransingh@hotmail.com

Hi, u don't know me, but I got your email id from Amarjitji. He has been a big help to all of us. I am Durga's sis-in-law. Obviously this is a blow for all of us. I wish I could come back but my baby is due any day now. I love Durga. Please look after her. She's been thru a lot. So have I, but at least I'm at home with my parents. If u're ever in Southall... u know who to contact. Cheers, Brinda.

PS. u can call me Binny.

To binnyatwal@gmail.com

Dear Binny,

It's wonderful to communicate with someone who knows Durga well, and cares for her. You can imagine how sad she is, and I am trying very hard to get her to speak to me. If there is anything you think will make her feel comfortable enough to talk, let me know. And of course, if there is anything you think I should know, let me know that too. Believe me, I will keep it confidential.

Do you have any family photographs? If you email them to me, it may be nice for Durga. Let us know when the baby comes along.

With best regards and thanks, Simran

TWO

It is true that my life is difficult to understand, and not many people can even hear me when I speak. If I don't leave here soon I will never be able to speak again. The memories keep swirling in my mind. What could I have done? Is there anything that can change things?

Yes, I will ask you to bring my books. My books which kept me alive and happy for so many years. I will read and be transported to another world, far away from that dark depressing house in Company Bagh. I remember the sweetness of those fantasies, which became more and more elaborate over time, spun out of my books. Someone would love me, someone would hold me close. Till one day, they became real.

When Sharda was detained in school for skipping a class, I stayed back too, so that we could go home together. I was her alibi, since she could later say that I had an extra lesson and she kept me company.

We crept into the library and opened up all the cupboards, even the shelves which we were not allowed to touch. As

an angry Sharda deliberately took out the forbidden books
on reproduction, on sexuality, she found copies of Lady
Chatterley's Lover, even a dog-eared copy of Geet Govinda,
and showed them to me, I tried to understand it all. This
was a world I knew nothing of—but as we turned the pages,
they enthralled us. It was almost as though we had discovered
another very secret world and were being launched on a voyage
of discovery. It was a warm, quiet afternoon, and as we giggled
our way through the books, we found ourselves getting flushed,
and very aware of each other, and because we knew each other
so well, there was little shyness. As we touched each other, I
remember laughing because everything was so funny, because
we were together and that was all that really mattered.

I understood some things that Sharda explained to me and
some I had no idea about, but as she told me what the books
said, I think I fell in love with her beautiful face, her eyes, her
lips all over again. She was no longer upset, she was smiling
and her body felt warm to my childish touch. Do you want to
see what you will be like one day? she asked me.

Sharda was so much older and I was a curious nine-year-old.
Under the desk in the library—the nuns were away in their
rooms—Sharda lifted up her skirt and closed her eyes. I was
almost clinical in my examination as she spread her legs and I
gazed upon the most beautiful triangle of hair. It was like an
anatomy lesson as I compared it to the drawing in the book,
and then Sharda gently took my hand and put it between her
legs and white sticky residue seemed to form. She asked me
to come closer and asked if I wanted to see her breasts. They
were white with brown nipples. As I touched them, I felt I had
never been so close to her before. It was a beautiful game.

Every one of those memories is attached to my books. We played other games as well. Often we would read stories of princes and princesses and enact them at home. I was the prince and Sharda was the delicate princess whom I would rescue. She became my idol—and even though I was much younger, I felt I had to protect her. We had always been a little isolated from everyone else and now there was a new reason to remain that way.

Sometimes we lay in bed, our arms wrapped so tight around each other that it was difficult to breathe. Till one day... well, what can I say? Things change, people change. Sharda was no longer interested in my lavish declarations of love. She was often missing from her bed at night. I missed her. And then she went away forever. Like everyone else.

I feel alone, as I have always been. The child who should never have been born anyway.

The files of newspaper clippings and other material related to the murders given to me by Amarjit's office weighed about six kilos. I staggered to an empty desk where I could read them peacefully. I wished I could smoke but no doubt it would create a scandal. This demure, bespectacled, saree-clad woman smoking—*chee chee chee*! It was another warm summer day, at least 40 degrees in the shade, and the jail compound was quiet, except for an occasional bell announcing the day's routine. The women inmates had been herded into various rooms for different activities which, piously but mistakenly, were meant to make them better human beings. As they cooked and cleaned and stitched, could they be drawn away from their terrible past? Or at least better adjusted to life outside the jail? If they ever left it.

I had spoken to Amarjit to see if we could get the sufi singer Imtiaz Ali to entertain them one day. He had looked at me as though I was quite mad. Why would they need any comfort or sense of normality? They were here to be punished, to repent, not to be entertained. Next I would be asking for air-conditioning and beauty parlours. I should concentrate on my case, not try for jail reforms, he said. In any case, I was only a voluntary worker, I had no authority to interfere, he said. These women were murderers and thieves. They had no pity for their victims. I should never forget that.

I opened the first file.

'Atwal case? I am the Superindent of Police here, Ramnath Singh.'

I looked up from the bloody photographs, bemused, at the slight man with suspiciously black hair combed right across his bald pate. He stood in front of me in full police regalia.

'Yes?'

'I've been asked to brief you. It's a very complicated case.' Ramnath sat down, uninvited, in front of me. He peered at the file from his upside down angle. 'Don't these photographs make you feel ill? If you had actually been to the house on that day... if I were to describe it to you...' He grimaced and stared away for a minute. He seemed friendly, if talkative.

'Please do. I met the girl yesterday. She seems quite traumatized. What do you think actually happened, Mr...?'

'Call me Ramnath. What do you know about her?' He sat down, checked his knife-edged trouser-crease and carefully crossed his legs. His polished black boots shone like twin headlights in the afternoon sun. He flicked open another file and glanced through it.

'Nothing much, really. She is fourteen, belongs to a wealthy family...'

'Very, very wealthy family.'

'Is studying... was perhaps raped.'

'We don't know if it was rape. There was definitely sexual intercourse.'

'Oh... did she... have a boyfriend?'

'They would have cut her throat if she did! So maybe she cut their throats before they could do it!' Singh laughed as he spoke. A slightly high-pitched whinny of a laugh.

I refused to get angry. Something about this very slick police officer made me uneasy. He reminded me of all the small-town men I had known; men who would look at a woman and quickly decide that she was a certain kind. I got the impression he was only being helpful because he had been told to be so—did he resent my entry into what should have been an open and shut case? And therefore, would he really be willing to share all his information with me? I was used to this reaction: people who knew who I was treated me like a social butterfly who had flown off-course temporarily, and would flit back to her five-star haunt soon enough.

'Then... who could have...?'

'These rich families are crazy.' He looked at me and paused deliberately, no doubt because he wanted to rub the point in. *Rich and crazy like you.* I did not rise to the bait. He continued, 'Anything is possible. Her sister died some years ago, that's another mystery. Died or disappeared. We never found the body.'

Ramnath gazed thoughtfully at the pictures in front of me.

'I wonder if they knew this was going to happen to them. Let me tell you. This is a huge seven-bedroom house with three verandas, a dining room, and a large courtyard. It's surrounded by gardens and fruit orchards. And in every room we found dead bodies. All her relatives—her father, mother, grandmother, two brothers, aunts, cousins. The servants had the weekend off to attend a wedding.

'There was blood everywhere. They found her the next morning with one of her hands tied to the bed. She was naked but alive.'

'So why was she brought here?'

'Circumstantial evidence. She bought the poison. Her fingerprints were on one of the knives that was used.'

'But her hands were tied, for god's sake.'

'Very loosely, and only one. Though there were marks and bruises all over her arms and she did tell someone initially, before she stopped talking to us, that both her hands had been tied. But there is just no other suspect and she can't tell us who the man, her alleged rapist, was.'

'She had also been poisoned.'

'That's easy enough. She could have had a bit—don't forget she's a clever girl—but not enough to kill her.'

Obviously, Mr Ramnath Singh had made up his mind about Durga, and very little would shake his belief.

'So what do you know about her?'

'She was a quiet girl. Most of the girls in her class go out, meet boys, see movies, etc. My daughters are in the same school. But she used to just go to school, and then go home. Not even to the movies. The car would drop her to school and pick her up after class.'

'And who do you think actually murdered the family?'

'That's the funny thing. We know she bought the poison because she went to a chemist's shop a few days earlier and said she needed some rat poison. And that's what was used to kill everyone. But...'

'What about all that blood?'

'Either the poison wasn't enough, and she had to use a knife, or maybe, yes, someone else was involved.'

'Couldn't it be someone else, entirely? Who then makes her the scapegoat?'

'What is the motive? Only she has the motive—she inherits everything, as the last surviving member.'

'A fourteen-year-old girl! It's difficult to believe.'

Ramnath got up. 'Talk to her. That's the best thing for all of us.'

'Doesn't she have any friends?'

'After her sister disappeared, the family kind of closed in. The only people she met at home would have been friends of her parents, or her tutor maybe, though that's doubtful because he stopped teaching her ages ago. One sister-in-law is in Southall. She was pregnant when she left, and is now too shocked to come back. They are worried about the baby.'

'What about the tutor?'

'Taught her literature, I believe. And computers. He is a much older man, father of a girl. We ran a check on him, seems clean and simple, doubt if there is anything there. He hasn't seen them for years, not after the sister vanished.'

'And the family, did you know them?'

'Oh, we all knew them very well. Very prominent, socially. Did a lot of charity in hospitals and schools. Very much into religion. Every Gurupurab they would have a big langar, and the raagis would sing for days in their house. The family retainer told us that there may have been a family quarrel and she may have gone berserk, she was very headstrong.'

I sank back with a sigh, watching him smartly half-march away, as though his knee joints had starch in them. Most of the information he had passed on was already available in the newspaper articles in front of me. There was only one way forward as far as I could tell. I would have to get Durga to talk to me. Mr Ramnath Singh would be only too happy to have me discover I was wasting my time and pack my bags for my next useless assignment.

That evening, when I entered the anteroom, she was already waiting for me. She was again dressed in a plain dark brown salwar kameez, her hair drawn severely back in a plait. Her eyes were puffy and red, she must have been crying. She gave me a quick glance and then looked away.

'So, how was your day?'

She shrugged.

'Did you write anything?'

She was quiet. She shook her head after a few moments.

'How are things for you here? Have you recovered from your injuries? You can tell me in complete confidence. I am like a blotting paper, I absorb everything but leak out nothing.'

A little joke to mellow her. She did not speak. Just the little tic at the corner of her mouth jumped.

'Durga, you haven't asked for a lawyer, you don't want to talk. How can anyone help you?'

'No one can help me.'

I was surprised at her voice. Today it was deep and truculent. She was not meek, she was angry.

'Of course I can. I have come to Jullundur especially for you, from Delhi.'

'Delhi?' She was startled.

'Are you familiar with Delhi?'

'No, I was supposed to go there very soon. Have you been to Lajpat Nagar?'

'Many times. Have you been there?'

'Someone I know lives there. I was going to visit... them.'

'On your own?'

'Is Delhi a nice place?'

'It's better than here, certainly. I ran away from Jullundur, you know!'

'Did you run away and get married?' A faint note of involuntary interest slipped into her voice.

'Oh no, some people run *away* from marriages. I was one of them!'

This time she almost smiled, but then that dark, grim look fell like a veil over her face.

'If you really want to help me... can you take me back to my house? I miss my room, my books.'

I was taken aback by her request. How could she want to go back to that house, wouldn't it rekindle disturbing memories? Or was she a lost child, looking for a source of comfort, an anchor, now that everything had been wiped out of her life? Perhaps she felt the house would heal her in some way.

'I'll try to get permission. What books would you like?'

'If you go to my room, you will find a shelf full of my school books. Will you bring those for me?'

In her brief glance at me was a terrible sadness, and I could see tears glinting in her eyes. Was that all she missed? What about her parents? Her brothers? Obviously I could not ask her.

'Brinda sends you her love. She sent me an email.'

It was Durga's turn to look surprised. A slow smile crept over her face.

'Has she had the baby?'

'Not yet.'

'Mandakini. She's going to call her Mandakini. Mandy.'

The road outside the jail was a haze of dust, and even though it was hot and sultry, I shivered. Perhaps it would rain later. I hailed a rickshaw, the best way to travel through the bumpy, congested streets, and asked the driver to take me to St. Mary's Convent.

I wondered if it had changed at all from the time I had studied there. It used to be the only 'English-speaking' school, where upwardly mobile parents could send their daughters. It was largely staffed by nuns from Kerala, whose black and white habits were a constant source of amusement. Another cause for laughter was the thick English accent of the Malayali nuns, which mingled not very happily with our Punjabi, creating a strange hybrid Mal-punj-lish understandable only to the inmates of the small world of St Mary's. 'No loffing and tokking' was the refrain most often heard, as they tried to groom us into yeng laddies. Studies were usually not a great concern (many of the girls, like me, had been parked there only to attract rich and handsome husbands).

Instead, in the hot afternoons with the sun streaming through the classrooms, we spent our time wondering whether the nuns wore any underclothes, whether they shaved their hair, and whether they were lesbians. In Jullundur, where nothing ever happened, the last great excitement had been the Partition of India a few decades earlier. Until terrorism arrived, most people drank their lassi and desi liquor quite peacefully. The Christian faith was completely alien, but to be approved of because it gave us a passport to English, and therefore a better life. There was little attempt at conversion. That was reserved only for the soft targets of the Church, the vulnerable Dalits, for instance, who lived on the margins of society. Converting to Christianity was a meal ticket for them: free education, health care and perhaps jobs. The more articulate could even hope for a lifetime in the service of the Vatican. Converting the middle class would have caused a scandal (though a few did convert, rather quietly, to the consternation of unsuspecting families). However, conversions lower down the social scale would not be noticed for many years to come.

As products of a hybrid culture, we ardently sang hymns and did a curious bobbing curtsey in church as we dipped our fingers in the holy water. The highlight was making the sign of the cross in front of the crucified figure of Jesus which nestled in Mary's heart, which in turn had burst open in bloody agony, dripping gorgeous ruby red drops of blood. The pain was almost delicious. Like strawberry ice cream.

Everything about the Christian faith made us aware of our own heathen upbringing, fed as we were on a diet of

Reader's Digest and *Women's Weekly*. Whilst we had to wear salwar kameez at home, we were allowed to wear skirts and shirts and even ties and blazers to school. Which meant we had to (secretly) shave our legs and make sure that our burgeoning breasts did not bounce too obviously in the tight white shirts. To even get razors in a Sikh household was a nightmare. It meant bribing the chowkidaar with extra sweets on every Guru's martyrdom day (yes, we celebrated the hacking of necks and gouging of eyes with delicious kara parshaad—wheat cooked in syrupy ghee) in the hope that he would keep our secrets if we kept him well-fed.

In school, we could have been mislaid dark-haired Irish progeny: we were taught to dance the Highland Fling and made to participate in elocution and theatre competitions. But funnily enough, at home no one asked me—or most of the girls I grew up with—to dance, or even wanted to hear an opinion from me. My father was too busy working, and my mother was too involved in flower decoration or the latest recipes. Schoolgirls like me had a curiously divided existence from which men, apart from those in the family, were firmly excluded.

The only time we interacted with a male outside the house was once a year when the nuns went into 'Retreat'. We were told they sought repentance for their sins and had taken a vow of silence. The air was rife with gossip over these 'sins'. Was Sister Margarita really a reformed cabaret dancer? And was Sister Catherine still meeting the soldier who used to love her till she joined the nunnery?

While they repented, in their place a priest would arrive to address us on 'personal matters'. For reasons we could never fathom, it was assumed that we would learn about sexuality from him. It was a bizarre ritual and, frankly, quite cruel to the hapless man. He was suddenly surrounded by a large possé of aggressive adolescent girls, or perhaps it was his dream come true!

It was assumed, I suppose, that being a man, he was better equipped to tell us the 'facts of life'. For once we were free to ask anything we wanted and since the questions were to be written on bits of paper and given in anonymously, they were all sexually charged. The two asked every year (passed down from one schoolgirl generation to another) were, 'What is a French kiss?' and 'Is it Unhealthy to Masturbate?' Once the two questions had been asked and we'd watched with glee the face of the priest slowly turning red (under his Kerala tan), a great sigh of joy would go around the room. He would begin to shake his knees in nervousness and glance around with the look of a trapped deer in the face of twenty determined hunters. We, meanwhile, would fix him with our beady eyes and refuse to giggle.

No doubt the Church sent these good men to us to stiffen their resolve and give them the courage to face far greater challenges than a bunch of frustrated Punjabi schoolgirls.

As I walked through the unchanged school gates, I remembered those turgid but exploratory years. A nun bounded towards me enthusiastically. She had been gardening, and her hands were covered with mud. I asked her if I could meet the principal and told her I was an old student.

The building was larger and better maintained than I remembered. Obviously the Church had more money now, even though its dominant status in education had been reduced in recent years with new, locally run schools springing up. These were no longer owned by religious institutions and were more secular, the better ones run by enterprising investors.

The principal, Sister Sarah, was in her office which was as spartan as it used to be, and was dominated by the iconic image of Jesus dripping blood on the cross.

My Hindu friends were used to plump happy gods or graceful voluptuous goddesses, but the Sikh iconography is much more gory, with several Sikh gurus and their families having been decapitated, impaled or butchered by the Mughals. No wonder temples are usually full of noise and clutter and dissonant music, while churches and gurudwaras are quietly awe inspiring and precisely orchestrated. Whenever we see images of torture, it is always in hushed silence and pain, isn't it? I resisted an impulse to dip a knee and cross myself.

Trophies lined one wall of the room. These were mostly for awards in the genteel arts which I remembered the school had been known for: acting, debating, elocution. Photographs of the head girls in their blue school skirts and white blouses hung near the door. All very neat and orderly.

Sister Sarah's desk was free of paper. A desktop computer sat to one side, incongruous beside her formal habit. A portly, dark woman, she had probably joined the school after I left, but she was visibly distressed when I told her the purpose of my visit.

'That poor child, what a tragedy, you know.'

'Can you tell me something about her? Was she a good student?'

'Quite good, you know, till her sister... disappeared. Up to that time her marks were reasonable, and we had found a nice tutor for the two of them. But after that, you know, she was... just about all right, you could say. Gave us no trouble at all. In fact, she was quiet as a mouse in class.' Sister Sarah's tone was rueful. 'We were shocked, shocked and horrified... you know.' The ubiquitous 'you know' was like a punctuation mark in her speech.

'Did you meet her parents?'

'Oh yes, she has been in our school since nursery. They came for every PTA. They were very polite, you know. Very orthodox. The mother was very religious, prayed all the time, you know. Poor soul.'

'But I have been told that Durga had no friends, never went anywhere.'

'She was very strictly brought up. Very quiet, used to read a lot.'

She clicked her computer on and rapidly scanned through some data. 'Here it is, her last report. It says she is a good student. Excellent at essay writing, full marks for her English. Excellent vocabulary. Overall scored eighty per cent in her exams. Gave us no trouble really.'

She turned away from the screen and sighed. 'So different from the others. Things are changing in Jullundur, you know. Girls are up to all sorts of things. Last year we had to expel two girls.' Sister Sarah stopped abruptly, hesitated as though she wanted to say something. Then, obviously changing her mind, she asked me if I wanted some tea.

While she rang for it, I looked around at the old photographs and a dim memory of Sister Josie surfaced. She had been the kindest among the nuns, the only one who did not hit the back of our knees with wooden scales, or make us run around the playground in the afternoon if we 'misbehaved' in class. She was young and pretty, and we sympathized with her because she could not endure the layers of clothes she had to wear and sometimes fainted in the hot sun. In fact, she received more than her share of 'punishment' to teach her humility. We would find her sometimes, in the evening, on her knees, scrubbing the filthy school toilets. One day there had been a terrible row when, despite being in quarantine, she had spoken to me. Someone, I still don't know who, told the Mother Superior. I was not allowed to talk to Sister Josie after that. Three years later, when I finished school, she stopped me at the staircase and whispered, 'Please forgive me, because I cannot forgive myself.' I knew exactly what she meant because by that time I had been thoroughly disgraced as well and bore the burden of a sinner. In that environment, it was pretty easy to change from a paragon of virtue to a cowering culprit. Sister Josie and I had parted on the same side of hell.

'What happened to Sister Josie?'

The face across the desk, only for a second, seemed to crumple and then it became as stiff as the white collar beneath her chin.

'She left the Church a few years ago, you know. And now, if you don't mind, I have a prior appointment,' she said gently. 'I think I will have to leave you now. I am sorry about the tea, perhaps some other time, you know?'

I don't know, actually, I wanted to say. I was going to offer her a cigarette to help her relax, then thought better of it. I came out of the office and walked around. The gardening nun was still leaping about, determinedly attacking the marigolds. I strolled towards the playground. How many hours had we spent there, playing basketball (of a kind), gathering for assembly or contorting our bodies in physical training sessions, which included gymnastics. My now stiff body could, at one time, summersault into the air and touch the ground gracefully, hands first.

The classrooms had obviously doubled in number, but there was an eerie sense of desolation, as though they had been evacuated in a hurry. I tried to imagine Durga walking in, a lonely figure, going to her class on the second floor. Sweat trickled down my back. The red evening sun threw large shadows of trees on the ground, and it was getting dark. Suddenly, I thought I heard Sister Josie calling me from one of the classrooms. I whirled around and saw a black robe cross the corridor, above.

My heart leapt. She was here! Sister Josie was still here.

I ran up the steps to the second floor, up to the nun standing by the library door. She turned around, she was smiling, but it was someone else. I wished her good evening and trembling from sorrow and confusion, left the school. I felt a huge weight upon me, and the old claustrophobia returned.

To simransingh@hotmail.com

Hi, thx for the news about Durga. What can I tell u? I was in Jullundur for barely six months. It was an arranged marriage—Jitu was supposed to come back with me—and b4 I could really settle down, I came away to have the baby. Durga was supposed to come later. Tell her Rahul remembers her. It will make her happy. When do u think they will release her?

Cheers, Binny

To binnyatwal@gmail.com

Dear Binny, who's Rahul? I am constantly getting mixed up with the large family. Though of course, now hardly anyone is left. Will give her the message.

Take care, Simran

THREE

My mother was very beautiful. I remember when she came to pick me up from school, one of the girls asked me if she was a film actress. She was tall and fair and my father was equally handsome. He looked like royalty, with a white flowing beard, which he would combine with dramatically coloured turbans. Together they looked like they had stepped out of one of Sahib Singh's paintings—you know, the artist who painted those famous but doomed lovers, Heer-Ranjha, Sohni-Mahiwal.

Though they looked made for each other, they were actually from different backgrounds. My mother's family was in the army—starting with the usual Genrail Singhs and Karnail Singhs (who were actually lowly Subedars) during World War I. Her father was named Major Singh and was the first one to actually reach that rank, many years later.

My father's family owned land spread out in small holdings. In Jullundur we were known for our blood-red strawberries. And for the nursing clinics we ran as charity.

My sister looked like my mother, she was equally lovely. My brothers were not as good-looking, but no one cared really, they were Boys and that was enough. We knew they were actually my cousins, but my father was crazy for sons, and so was my mother. So they got all the attention. I was never anywhere among the beautiful people. I was dark, and very hairy. Too much perhaps, for a girl. Maybe I had been given the wrong diet, or my testosterone levels were too high. My earliest memories are of my ayah Amla oiling me and letting me run around in the sun. In fact, most people thought I was her child, as I grew progressively darker and darker till I was the colour of soot, which was Amla's colour. Then one day my mother condescended to look at me and she was horrified to see the dark, ugly, bristly little creature I had become. They began to massage me daily with besan mixed with curds in slow circular motions so that the hair would lessen, and I would turn fair.

No such luck.

I was meant to be the 'kala teeka'. It is said that if everything goes well, the wrath of the gods descends on you, so you have to put a black mark somewhere on your body to deflect misfortune. I was the black mark for the Atwal family.

As I grew up, the regular applications of Fair and Lovely and hydrogen peroxide turned the dark hair all over my body into a more acceptable blond fuzz.

But there were other things which were not so easy to resolve. I began to notice strange things around the house. Even though I was much more of a boy than a girl (at least in my own mind) and I was always climbing trees and breaking my bones, I was never treated with the same sort of respect the Boys got. I tried to do everything they did, including horse-

riding and cricket. I even learnt to smoke (which no Sikh family could tolerate) and abuse like them, but all I got were slaps, and all they got was love and praise. Even their smoking was shrugged off as a childish prank. It was a chasm that I could not cross: I had longer hair than theirs, and so I would tie mine in a turban, wear their trousers and shirts, but no one seemed to appreciate any of it. All they would do was look at me and sigh and say, 'Poor thing, no one will ever marry her.'

I did not understand why I had to be married. Why couldn't I stay in this Bhoot Bangla of a house for ever and ever? My brothers would be married and they would bring home a bahu each. I also dreamt of bringing home a lovely blushing bahu for my mother. Perhaps then she would like me.

I asked my sister to marry me so that neither of us would ever have to leave the house. It was the best solution. I think she cried that day.

The TV channels were reporting Durga's case again. Someone had tracked down her sister-in-law in Southall.

'Can you tell us about Durga?' The microphone was thrust at Brinda Atwal, alias Binny. I looked at her curiously. She had a typical cockney-Brit accent but the rest of her was very traditional. Lovely long black hair, a very appropriate white salwar kameez. She was sharp featured and attractive, the only colour on her face a dash of bright red lipstick. The background showed a middle-class terraced British home with lace curtains in the windows and a large, framed cross-stitch tapestry of Guru Nanak emanating rays of light from his hand straight onto her.

'Poor thing. I am very fond of her, really.'

'Did you get a hint of this... that she might do this?'

'Look, I don't think she did anything. She's completely innocent. She's only fourteen years old, after all. You know what the justice system in India is like. I worry about her all the time. I believe *and* I know she's done nothing wrong and yet she's the one they've caught. The real culprits are probably out there, walking free.'

'Can you describe her, and the family?'

'I didn't know them very well. It was an arranged marriage. I've lived in Southall all my life, I was born here. Durga's brother Jitu was going to come back with me. We had just got married in January...'

'What about your in-laws?'

'They were all right. They were very strict, very god-fearing. My mother-in-law was always praying and going to the gurudwara... I really don't think they had any enemies. They seemed to be very close to each other. And very well integrated into Jullundur's society. People liked them. They respected them.'

'So what happened?'

'I don't know, as I said. And Durga is in judicial custody now, so I haven't been able to speak to her recently, but I am in touch with her through a social worker, Simran Singh.'

'But your baby has lost a father...'

Binny took a deep breath, and something flickered on her face. 'We'll manage, somehow. I think... everything happens for the best.'

'What do you mean?' The reporter sounded shocked.

Binny looked straight into the camera. 'I mean that if the child had to lose her father, it is better this way, because she won't feel the pain. You can't miss someone you never knew.'

As the news bulletin switched to politics, I sat back with my cup of coffee and cigarette, alone in the privacy of the guesthouse, impressed with the stoic, calm answers from Binny. I would call her one of these days.

So Binny was going to provide British residency for Jitu. Everywhere in Punjab, hundreds of families happily give up their daughters and sons for a foreign passport. The value of their sons, especially in pounds and dollars, is far more than in rupees and besides, they would earn much more as taxi drivers and cleaners in the UK than they ever would at home. In case no legal route or suitable bride is found, the boys become 'kabutars' or 'pigeons', a euphemism for the thousands of illegal Punjabi males who surface on a beach in Europe or the US, smuggled in by sea or by air. They are often close to death, and starving—but in true Punjabi spirit, they find a Punjabi link and disappear into an unfamiliar land, forever. Another way is to bring in very young children from a village and simply forget to send them back. They grow up in homes where they lead lives very similar to those back in Punjab—the same language, the same prayers, the same clothes. The only difference is the weather, and a promise of a Western education. Passports are then mysteriously found with the children's names on them and over the years the tired, abused system of these welfare-oriented countries find more names added to their list of citizens.

Had he lived, Jitu would have used the easier route. Looking through the files, it appeared that he had managed an impressive third division in college. He was 'BA pass', again an important qualification. Once upon a time, his wealthy family background would have allowed Jitu to live off the fat of the land.

However, the Atwals were not immune to the declining returns from agriculture, squeezed to a trickle by the ruinous impact of multiple crops and pesticides, and the rising cost of farming. Slowly land was being swallowed up for more lucrative and less uncertain businesses than agriculture, or it was being divided up for building homes.

Though the Atwals had not hit rock bottom as far as their wealth was concerned, Jitu was only a nephew and would not inherit the major chunk of the property. It was a familiar landscape of accumulating reasons for him to find a 'phoren' bride.

Similarly, in the UK, a girl like Binny, after she had tried her first drink, had her first boyfriend, worn her first mini-skirt and lost her virginity, would be wrapped in a red bridal saree and parcelled off to a traditional family. Her parents would have dreamt of this since she was born. And from that moment onwards, her British modernity would be carefully concealed beneath her red silk dupatta. It would never reappear. The perfect combination: Kudi from UK marries Pind da Puttar. Or vice versa. All the problems that followed concerned no one and no one would ever resolve them. Till a macabre incident like a multiple murder took place and suddenly the kaleidoscope shifted. Was Jitu's immigration also related to the murders in some way?

Outside my room I could see another hot evening lurching up, pushing its fiery fists into the still air. There was no sign of winter yet. Normally, by this time I would be at home in Delhi with my mother, shopping for Diwali presents and diyas to light the house with, but this year, I wanted to spend time unravelling Durga's case. Perhaps, it occurred to me, I could get special permission from Amarjit to take Durga to her home for Diwali. It might release the pent-up emotion within her, it might even be the trigger that helped her to finally speak.

The more I thought about it, the more I liked the idea. But before that I still felt the need to learn something more about the 'suspect'. I went through the list of phone numbers of my school friends who might still be around and, on the fifth try, I managed to find Amrinder Bains.

Amrinder and I had been rivals at St Mary's. If I topped a subject one time, Amrinder had to equal the score in the next test. I had thought she would become a great scientist or a mathematician. But she had chosen to stay at home and look after her sick mother, which was how I managed to track her down, by her mother's address. The doughty Ma Sukhi could blow out candles by just inhaling and could suck out your oxygen faster than anyone else I knew. I felt a remembered pang of nervousness at the thought of meeting her and Amrinder again: the last time we met, it had not been very pleasant. But perhaps things would be different now. After all, Amrinder was married and had two daughters. One of them was in Durga's class.

I called for a cycle rickshaw and was soon back on the road. The sight of the rickshaw puller's skinny legs peddling away made me wish I could have walked, but that would be an invitation to be teased by the Roadside Romeos, that peculiar species of Indian male which prefers to abandon all other activity in favour of a boisterous attack on unsuspecting women of all ages. Even though I was no 'spring chicken' (in my mother's acerbic view), I did still attract an occasional second glance. So I decided to sit back and enjoy the rarity of the rickshaw ride.

Unfortunately, my reverie was shattered by a bus that spat a funnel of petrol breath in my face as it went past. I pulled my dupatta over my head and sat for the rest of the journey with my knees drawn up, all hunched over. Altogether, not a very graceful entry to make into polite Jullundur society.

When I got to Amrinder's house, I was surprised to see a police jeep standing outside. And even more astonished to spot Ramnath Singh getting out.

'We meet again!'

'I believe you were in school with my wife. I wish you had told me, I would have invited you over yesterday itself.'

Somehow I had not associated a cold fish like Ramnath with Amrinder. But then, I hadn't even asked her about her husband.

'A simple explanation, then. I thought you had come to arrest her!'

'She is already under house arrest, as you can see,' he replied in his over-familiar, bantering tone, accompanied by that annoying laugh, as Amrinder emerged. Much larger than I remembered her, but still very pretty, with the long brown hair now trimmed into a fashionable bob.

'Hi. I thought you knew. We got married straight after school. One slight warning before we go in—Mother has cancer, but she doesn't like to talk about it. She is asleep right now, but she might want to meet you.' Amrinder took me to the sitting room, while Ramnath went into their bedroom to pack. He was going away for a few days to Amritsar.

There had been an explosion on the Samjhauta Express, the historic train which ran between Lahore and New Delhi. The bomb was suspected to have been planted by the ISI, or Al-Qaeda, or even SIMI. There are so many militant organizations being nurtured in India that the police can cherry-pick a name and arrest anyone. They were still counting the dead, and hospitals were flooded with the wounded.

Amrinder's house, like all the others in Model Town, was large and spacious, with a carefully landscaped garden. The heavily embellished baroque balcony overlooked the garden and the front road, and it was all done in ice pink, a favourite colour in Jullundur where most of the houses were either ice pink, or sea blue, or mint green. The idea being perhaps that the lighter the colour, the more quickly it would require repainting, and what better way to demonstrate your wealth than by getting your home redone more often than the neighbours did? The house was overcrowded with cut-glass and imported porcelain figures and the furniture was all velvet Victoriana, with golden arms and legs. Ramnath was obviously doing well and had married well too. I was hoping he would leave soon, and not sit with us. I had an unpleasant feeling he had come home only to find out why I was meeting Amrinder after so many years. Was he going to eavesdrop?

Amrinder had already laid the coffee table with fresh lime juice and home-made chocolate cake. For a few moments I forgot the rivalry that had dogged us through our school years.

'It's been, what, twenty years since we met?'

'Remember how hard we used to compete with each

other? It was such a joke!' She laughed, flashing her perfect white smile. I kept my lips firmly shut over my nicotine stained teeth. I didn't quite look back at our school days with laughter but right now I wanted to keep this meeting as pleasant as possible.

'So how has it been to come back after so many years?' Amrinder asked, still keeping her tone light. If any memories were flooding back, as they were for me, she kept them on a tight leash.

'I don't know if I would have come back if Amarjit hadn't asked me to help with Durga. I've been trying to get to know her, I even went back to the school to try to get some clues. But frankly, apart from the newspapers and the TV reports, I know hardly anything about her.'

'Ram is very keen to close the case. She is the prime suspect, you know.'

'But she's also very young, and is showing the classic symptoms of trauma. She seems all closed in. So I thought I should ask you; you've been here a long time. Your mother and daughters would all know her and the family as well.'

'I don't know how much Ram has told you...'

'Look, we hardly got a chance to talk. Why don't you tell me whatever you know? It might be the only way to help the girl.'

'Help the girl? Who would want to help a murderer?' Amrinder sounded aghast.

'My job is to get her to talk. She was poisoned, tied up, raped, terrorized. Her whole family is wiped out.' I looked for some sign of sympathy but it was like squeezing blood from a stone. Magically, before me surfaced the obdurate, ambitious, self-obsessed girl Amrinder used to be. Now, as the wife of a senior police officer in a small town, she was even more irritatingly smug. I was no longer surprised that they had married each other. A perfect match.

'Did Ram tell you about her sister?'

'Yes.'

'Look, my gut feeling is, it is a blighted family, there is very little you will be able to do. But I think that the two things are connected. The first daughter disappearing, and now this.'

'What do people say about her sister?'

'They say she was pregnant and disappeared. She was sixteen. I think she went a little crazy.'

'How long ago was this?'

'Five years.'

'Durga would have been only nine years old then.'

'That's right... but she knew something. And maybe she didn't forgive the family. The two sisters were very close.'

'And do you think that one of them... the father, the brothers, could have been involved with the sister's disappearance?'

'That Jitu was capable of anything. If the family wasn't so well known, that boy would have been in prison. Absolute badmaash. I think he was a cousin, not a real brother.'

Before I could ask my next question, Ramnath came out, ready to go, followed by two girls, who surprised me with their air of modernity. As he left, I realized that obviously Ramnath's unspoken criticism of women did not extend to his daughters, who were being groomed into certain aneroxia and escape from Jullundur. They had Liverpool or Birmingham stamped on their foreheads in neon lights. Their short hair was fashionably streaked, and their thin bodies were squeezed into jeans and tight T-shirts. No doubt the next forty years of their lives had been carefully planned by their parents who themselves had not been able to leave this town.

One of them was planning to become a doctor, Amrinder told me, and the other was going to study computer science. Along the way, they would get married. She kept it casual, but she did not forget to mention that they both had gold medals in academics. And of course, they could sing at a near classical level. Another five minutes and I would have drowned in the sea of their virtues. It was always essential to play up the talents of your daughters because, in Punjab, many people would wonder how you could live without sons. Yet, for no fault of theirs, I felt my dislike of the parents pass onto them. I tried to keep it from showing on my face and smiled as warmly as I could.

'Did you know Durga?' I asked them.

Reena, who was in the same class as Durga, made a face. 'She is a real behenji. You know, always in a salwar kameez, trying to be terribly straight, and look what she did!'

The younger daughter, Sangeeta, spoke up slowly: 'I think that whole family is strange. They used to keep such a strict watch on her, she wasn't allowed anywhere. I mean, our parents are also strict, but we can go out once in a while on our own. To be fair, Durga did very well at school, her essays were always read out to us, but like... she was not even allowed to stay for school functions.'

'I think it became worse after her sister vanished. When we were younger, she was quite a tomboy, she was always playing cricket with her brothers. She would insist on wearing trousers or shorts like them, outside school. Weird.'

'Did you try to get her to come out and visit or play together?'

'I used to call her over for birthday parties. She came for a few when she was younger but no, I can't say we tried very hard. She was almost invisible in school, except for her writing, no one really bothered with her. I mean, there's so much classwork, tests, homework, and then you have your own friends. If someone isn't available, you kind of forget about them.' Reena was equivocal.

'And do you remember her older sister?'

'I don't, not much, but some of my friends do, and they said she was very beautiful but, you know, a bit free with the boys.'

Amrinder raised her eyebrows. 'Who told you that? And where would she have met the boys?'

Reena blushed. 'It's just gossip, Ma.'

I left soon after, as mystified as before. Even as I stepped out of the door, I could hear Amrinder's high-pitched voice taking Reena to task. Where had she heard this gossip? Who had told her?

I knew the Atwal house was in Company Bagh, a remnant of the old colonial East India Company days. Anyway, nothing in Jullundur is more than twenty minutes apart, even at the remarkable speed of five kilometres per hour that I seemed to be travelling at.

As the rickshaw turned on to Company Bagh, I could see the house looming up ahead, next to a defunct car showroom. There was a disused well near the entrance and, just as Ramnath had described it, the house towered over the surrounding buildings. It was painted a dull yellow (not ice pink, thank god) and all the windows and doors were closed. There were two policemen at the door, and after I had identified myself and they had confirmed it on their handsets, I was allowed to walk in through the front veranda.

What had I expected? The house looked and smelt ancient. It grew like a tree out of the earth, completely rooted. There was nothing impermanent about it.

If it was a blighted house, it must have been blighted for centuries, for aeons. The plants outside seemed defiantly healthy for such a desolate house; perhaps the servants were still around. I struggled with one of the heavy wooden doors with its wire-mesh shutters and finally opened it, to the amusement of the two guards. In true Punjabi macho style, they did not shift a muscle to help me. If I needed help, I had to ask for it. But being a stubborn Dilliwali, I would not ask. Those days were gone.

Inside, the house had been swept clean. Apart from the dustcovers on the furniture and the paintings, nothing seemed to have been moved in the recent past. Yet, there was a disturbance in the air, like in a garden when the birds have just taken flight and everything, even the little mites in the air, seem to be alert and waiting. Was it my imagination or was it a house in anticipation of something or someone? I was reminded of those ghostly scenes from old black and white films like *Madhumati* when the actor goes into an isolated home and discovers his past life. The thought made me smile, because certainly I felt no connection or sense of familiarity about the house. I began to lift away the dustsheets to see what was beneath, half prepared for a dismembered hand to fall out, an eyeball to roll down, or blood stains on the upholstery. But there was no trace of the recent massacre. If there had been any, it had been washed out and cleaned. The bloodbath of thirteen people could have been a passing shower. Yet, I thought the smell was still there, of slightly putrid flesh, and there were charred and blackened streaks on the wall, from the unsuccessful attempt to torch the house. Or perhaps it was only my imagination.

I moved on, carefully looking at all the family pictures on the wall. Durga's parents were very good-looking, which somehow reinforced the image I had of them of being soft-spoken and genteel. It was peculiar that, while everyone had told me how respected they were, no one had mentioned their outstandingly handsome faces, patrician with their steady calm gaze, used to instant obedience. They had not looked so well-dressed or groomed with their pearl strings and diamond cuff-links at the time of their death. The photographs I had seen in the police station were of bloodied, maimed bodies—quite unrecognizable, if I compared them to these grand compositions.

There were plenty of black and white as well as colour photographs and posed portraits. The two boys were also there. The older one had to be Jitu, he looked in his mid-twenties. Close by was a larger portrait of him and Brinda on what must have been their wedding day. Jitu was in full wedding gear, complete with a sword dangling by his side. Brinda sat half turned towards the camera with a shy smile, her bright pink and gold duppatta trailing the floor. You could see the mehndi on her hands, traced in delicate patterns, between the silver kaleeras and the red chooda. She was almost smothered in gold jewellery—large obscene chunks dangled from her ears and covered her chest like armour.

Strangely, there weren't any photographs of either Durga or her sister. There were a few other portraits of men and women, probably other family members, but it was as though the two girls had never existed. I walked through the house, opening and shutting doors, and found nothing that reminded me of Durga. Perhaps there would be a photo album somewhere.

Behind me, I heard a door open. But maybe it was only the breeze pushing at the doors and windows. I could hear the dogs barking in the distance. Were they on the premises? Someone had mentioned that one of the three dogs had died on the night of the murders, poisoned like the rest.

'Who's there?' I shouted out. I went to the window and opened it to call the guards. But they were busy talking and would not look towards me. Chastizing myself for being nervy, I walked back to what I thought was Durga's room. It still had some stuffed toy animals, and the desk was covered with books. On one side, precariously perched under a dustcover, was a computer with a state-of-the-art printer. She must need the latest technology for her school work, if she was studying computer science. On the shelf over her bed, just as she had said, were her school books. I took down a few—literature, chemistry, mathematics. Curiously, putting the chosen books on the bed, I began to explore the room. There had to be something here. Something that would reveal the mystery behind Durga and her family. I opened each drawer in the desk. Nothing but the usual requirements for school, some pens and pencils. I opened up notebooks, many of them in Gurmukhi, and shook them out, then skimmed through the pages. Did she have a diary? Where could she have kept it?

I opened the cupboards but there was nothing in them. No clothes. Only a few dusty newspapers, and two hangers.

I felt around the bed. Under the mattress was a very slight bump. I put my hand in and pulled out what seemed to be a bunch of papers. I saw to my dismay that they too were in Gurmukhi. All those years when I should have learnt the script of Punjab and had refused, just to defy my parents! I stuffed the papers in my handbag, not feeling the least bit guilty about removing evidence, because I knew that once I managed to decipher them, they would go to Ramnath or Amarjit.

'Are you looking for something special?' A thin, slightly stooped man in a kurta pyjama stood at the door. He spoke to me in Hindi, not Punjabi, with a distinct Bihari Bhojpuri lilt. 'Are you from the police?'

'No! Well, yes, I am with the police.' I jumped up hastily and began to pick up the books, after settling the mattress down again. 'I met Durga at the jail, and she asked for these books.'

'What will she do with these books, that foolish girl! Books have ruined her life and she still thinks she needs them.' He was scathing in his recrimination. 'So she meets you. Did she tell you how she killed them?'

'No... we don't know that. Who are you?'

'I have worked in this house for forty years, and it is my misfortune that I wasn't killed that night. I wish I had gone with sahib and memsahib, what is the point of living now? Durga, why did you do this...' Tears began to stream from his eyes. 'I have nowhere to go now. This was my home, where do I go now?'

He glared at me, then as abruptly as he had come in, he began to walk away.

'No, wait, stop. Tell me more about Durga.'

'I will not talk about that snake child. We should have killed her when she was born. She ate her parents... they were...' He stopped to wipe his tears.

'What about her parents?'

'He was a saint, a complete saint. They never knew what those snake children were doing.'

'What happened to her sister?'

'She was a snake too. Who knows? Who knows? I have to go now.'

He pulled his arm away even as I anxiously grasped it.

'What is your name?'

'Manubhai.'

I watched him leave, helplessly. Everyone seemed to know much more than I did, but somehow I had to keep plodding on till all the pieces came together.

'Wait!' I called after him. 'Where are all the photographs of Durga and her sister?'

'She tore them all up, two, three years ago. She has a terrible temper and when she gets angry, it's the end of the world.'

'Why did she get angry?'

'With her parents. She was always fighting with them. Let me go now. I have work to do.'

'Can I see you another time?'

He waved at me dismissively and went towards the courtyard, and I followed him, relieved to leave the dark, suffocating house. It was a house of death all right. As I placed the rest of the books in my handbag, a photograph fell out. It was an unexpected picture of a naked girl, her face half hidden by a swathe of thick black hair. It did not look like Durga.

❧

To binnyatwal@gmail.com

Hi it was great to see you on TV. You look well, and very pregnant! I went to the house today but the funny thing is I didn't find a single photograph of Durga or Sharda. Do you have any idea where they could be? Manubhai says they were all torn up. Do you know anything about Durga's tutor? I thought I should meet him.

Take care, Simran

To simransingh@hotmail.com

Hi am due to check into the hospital soon. I'll email u the photographs when I get back. Are u on facebook, its easier that way. I never met Durga's tutor, sorry. Ask Durga about Rahul. I think she shd tell u, not me. Am attaching a news clip from today's *Daily Mail*. Makes me mad, but what do we do.

Binny

FOUR

12/9/07

Trying to be a girl is not easy. There are few comforts that you are born with or can attain. I know, they dress you in frocks and put ribbons in your hair, bangles on your arms, anklets on your feet, teach you to sing and dance and bake cakes, but what about the Inside-you? The Outside-you can smile and cut vegetables and sit with legs crossed and say 'namaste auntie' but the Inside-you is always angry and looking out of the window and wanting to run with the Boys.

The Boys did not have to go to a convent school, they went to a proper co-educational boarding school where they learnt to smoke and drink, but my sister and I had to be 'got ready for marriage'. My sister was, I think, cleverer than the Boys. She was a good business woman, too. She could look at the stocks and shares in the business programme on television and tell us which ones were going to go up, and which were not. She would study the trends over a few weeks and then make a complicated chart and my father would then invest in the shares. But who got the shares? Not she. They were all put in the name of the Boys. Nothing ever came to my sister because she, like me, was paraaya dhan. Amla explained the concept of paraaya dhan to me. It meant basically that girls were wealth, but wealth which belonged to someone else, i.e., the husband. The man who would come one day, with a lot of music and dance and take the wealth away. From what I could gather, all this would happen quite soon, because girls were like horses: the young fillies were easier to manage than the older ones. And the younger they were, the more they were in demand.

My sister was like me on the Inside. She wanted us never to leave, to stay close to each other. Also, we had just learnt that next door, the girl who had gone away as a bride had come back as a corpse within a month, she had been burnt because her dowry had been insufficient. We cried to Amla that we did not want to be paraaya dhan. Couldn't we become Boys? Boys were safe, they got shares, they did not have to leave their homes.

There was no point going to my mother because she had already told us that we were going to be married as soon as we were old enough. My father had also told us that no girl in the family had ever worked and there was no reason for him to educate us beyond school.

What if we were burnt for dowry? There were no answers. My father was rich, but if he could not even put a single share in my sister's name, how could he save her life?

The headlines on television announced that saplings were being planted in memory of all the 'disappeared daughters'.

Punjab is known for murdering its daughters. The sex ratio here is the lowest in the country—less than 850 girls per 1000 men—and despite all sorts of dire warnings from social scientists and demographers, girls are still considered inauspicious. In Chandigarh, the über urban capital that Punjab shares with Haryana, it is now 777 per thousand males. In some villages of Haryana it is a miserable 370. Delhi is also fast reaching those dismal figures. I thought of trees being planted all over the concrete mass of the city—and all the cities of the country. The bright life-affirming green against the dead grey of the cityscape. Trees pushing out of windows, bedrooms, school rooms, offices, toy shops, bridal parlours, empty cradles... green leaves left like tiny footprints everywhere the girls would have been, had they lived.

Not so long ago, the midwives used to take away newborn girls from their mothers, seal them in earthen pots and roll the pot around till the baby stopped crying. Or they would simply suffocate them. Or give them opium and then bury them. For a largely farming community, girls were a burden.

Why was I so angry? Binny had just sent me a news clip about a fifty-nine-year-old British woman (name withheld for privacy, of course) of Indian origin who had come to India along with her seventy-two-year-old husband. From Wolverhampton, of course. After expensive IVF treatment, she swanned back to the UK, only to dump her twin daughters in a hospital. She didn't want them. Of course. The reason? She had wanted sons. Oh, of course. Why didn't I think of that? Damn. I couldn't get the image of the children out of my head. It doesn't matter where you live, or how old you are. You can be educated, middle class, British, but your longing for a son will never leave you... Bloody murderers. I wanted a beer desperately. I needed to cool down.

I was back in my room, barely recovered from my visit to the house in Company Bagh. I had to meet Durga this evening, so I had to calm down. Yet, at the same time, I could not stop thinking of all the insecurities of being female. Hadn't things changed? Shouldn't I be more upbeat? We had had a woman prime minister, we had a woman president, we had women representatives everywhere. But had things really changed? This morning I had yet again read about a woman being branded a witch, then stripped naked and paraded around a village in Uttar Pradesh.

I took out the photograph of the girl that I had found at the house and looked at it closely. She was lying on a bed, but was she asleep? Who was she? I turned over the picture, but found nothing on the other side. There was no name, no date. It was certainly not a pornographic photograph. Nor was it posed. The camera angle was somewhat disquieting—you could not see the room at all. The way the girl was lying was artless, she did not know she was being photographed. Something about the way she lay on the bed was unnatural, stiff, as though she had been 'arranged'... was it a bed? In the foreground was the edge of a window or a door. Or was it a cell? Was the shadow the bar of the cell? But why was the girl lying like that? I put the photograph on the scanner and enlarged it. I clicked it to a larger and larger size till it pixellated and broke into a million fragments. Yes, as I feared... among the pixellated broken pieces were the girl's eyes. Wide open, staring sightlessly at the ceiling.

Why did Durga have this photograph hidden amongst her books? Was this why she had sent me there and why she asked me for the books? I had a hunch that it could be the missing sister, but who could I show a photograph like this to? What if Durga had not meant for me to find it? In any case, even my feeble counselling skills told me not to show it to Durga just yet, as she was already distressed. It might make her retreat further. This case was going nowhere very fast, anyway. If I did not rush in with more evidence, it would not really matter. I had already been here for four days, and all I had was a long list of questions... and a deafening silence.

I glanced through the set of Gurmukhi papers picked up from the house. I decided to get a simple Gurmukhi primer and decipher them for myself, before I gave them up.

But first, I would go to the city and pick up some liquor for the night, so I could sleep properly. I was beginning to get anxious.

On the way, my mobile phone rang. It was one of the rare occasions when I had forgotten to switch it off. It was my mother.

'Are you okay?' she wanted to know. 'Have you been back to see your old home?'

'No, been too busy with this case. I met Amrinder, she is married to a police officer, two lovely girls.'

There was a pained silence at the other end. My mother hated any mention of the M word. It reminded her that she could have been knitting booties for her grandchildren, instead of looking after a gin-swilling, cigarette-smoking forty-five-year-old renegade daughter who never grew up. She also hated the mention of Amrinder, since it re-opened a sorry chapter in our lives she wanted to close forever.

'Will you be home for Diwali?'

'It's a long way off, mom. Why don't you go ahead and fix something with your friends?'

'I think I'll just have a quiet evening at home. There has been another bomb explosion in Delhi. Al-Qaeda, I believe. Or the Huji. Or the Harkat something or the other. No one really knows. It could be a Bangladeshi group or a Pakistani group or a Kashmiri group. No one wants to celebrate. These damn suicide bombers are a complete nuisance.'

My mother is a master of the understatement.

Fifty people killed in Amritsar. It could be the return of terrorism... The rickshawallah who wanted to get home early had told me the casualty figure in the train explosion.

As we spoke, I thought of Durga. Actually, she was another kind of suicide bomber—if she really had killed her family—because she would have known she would get caught. Why had she made it so obvious? Why hadn't she run away? Not a very clever thing to do, was it, to stay on? To be seen buying the poison? But then suicide bombers like to take the credit through their suicide tapes. The only hitch with this explanation was the fact that Durga had been raped. No matter how smart she was, that would have been tough to arrange.

I placated my mother by promising to be home soon. She could not reconcile herself to the fact that, apart from not getting married and all the other sins I was guilty of, I also had to get involved with murderers. Why couldn't I, at the very least, enjoy kitty parties at the Gymkhana club? My mother loved these ritual monthly get-togethers with her married or idle unmarried friends in which each one of them put a fixed sum of money into the 'kitty'. There would be a lottery and whoever won the 'kitty' threw a lunch for the losers. The venue changed and the money deposited increased or decreased according to the wealth of the players. Up the rich-list ladder, the lunch venues got more and more elaborate and the conversation less and less interesting. Someday I must find out why no one ever got the terrible pun behind calling it a 'kitty' party.

I told her, as gently as possible, that I would miss her kitty party this month. I could sense the full weight of her disappointment as she said goodbye. Hey bhagwan, what had she ever done to deserve me?

With a real sense of urgency now, I got into my chariot and asked the shocked rickshawallah to take me to the nearest 'Indian Made Foreign Liquor' (another anachronism) shop. Feeling slightly more cheerful after having bought some gin, whisky and beer, despite the peculiar looks I got from the shop attendant, I disguised them in brown paper bags. Then, after dropping them off at the guesthouse, I headed back to the remand home and, settling down in the anteroom, waited for Durga.

Today she was back in her blue suit and her hair had been washed, so it was still open. It was really very long. I thought of the photograph I had found at the Company Bagh house and wondered if it was her, after all.

'I brought you your books. I just picked up whatever I could carry but if there is anything you'd prefer, tell me, I can always go back.'

She looked puzzled as she took the books from me. 'These are not my books.'

'What? But I got them from your room.'

'See.' She opened the front page, and I was surprised that I had not noticed. Both in Gurmukhi and in English, prettily curled letters spelt out 'Sharda'.

'These are my sister's books.'

'But I looked all over. It was the only room that looked like it was yours.'

Her eyes filled with tears. 'They've taken away my books. When Sharda... disappeared, they hid everything of hers. Now I am not there... they've taken away everything. Did you find anything else at all?'

I thought of the photograph but hesitated to mention it. So I shook my head.

She covered her face. Her near silent sobs sounded desolate, as though her last hope had been extinguished. I wondered who she meant when she said 'they'. After all, there was no one left in that house any more. Her family was all dead.

'Listen. Let me describe the room to you. It is the third door after the dining room, and there is a desk with a computer...'

She took her hands away from her face, slowly. 'That is my room,' she said, looking surprised. 'But where are my books? Ma'am, please, I need to read something, do something, keep my mind alert, otherwise, in here, I shall go mad.'

'Look, I will ask permission to take you back there, maybe a little before Diwali. You may want to light a lamp for your family, in remembrance...'

She was disbelieving. 'They will never allow it.'

Again the mysterious 'they'. Did she think her family had been resurrected? Or was she living in a make-believe world? Or did she mean the police? I did not want to question her right now.

'I don't know why you say that. We are here to help you. You've been through a very traumatic period. We need to help you understand what happened, and then we need to bring closure to it and move on.'

There was no doubt in my mind that she was a very intelligent girl. She knew exactly what I was saying. In a sense, I was also gambling on using this chance to build a relationship between us, something that would make her trust me, and then perhaps we could talk.

'Tell me about your sister. What was she like?'

'She was very beautiful.' Durga traced the letters of the name inscribed on the book with her fingers. My eyes went to the tattoo on her arm.

'Whose name is that?'

'It's not a name,' she replied.

She kept quiet, but I leaned forward to try to read it. It looked like the alphabet 'S'. Or it could have been a snake, draped around a heart. It was obvious she did not want to talk about it.

'I believe you burnt all the photographs in the house of her and you? There were no pictures when I went there.'

'I burnt the photographs? I did no such thing. Who told you that?'

'Someone I met at the house... Manubhai.'

'What a liar. They are all liars. They do things and blame me because that is the easiest thing to do. Especially now. Even if they told you that I used to drink the blood of cows and sit on a broomstick and fly, you would believe it. What about me? I was beaten, I was poisoned, I was raped, but no, that is unimportant.'

Durga's rage was apparent, but she did not look at me. She was still addressing the floor.

'Durga, tell me what made you angry when you were at home.'

'Everything and everyone. There was no meaning to anything. There should be joy and happiness and beauty in everything we do... but in that house, especially after Sharda left, there was nothing. Nothing to care for.'

'Your mother was very religious?'

'Oh yes... but only recently. Before that it was all parties and club nights. Then some bad things happened and she decided only God could understand.'

'Your brothers...'

'The boys. Yes, the boys. I was one of them too. But they didn't want me around once I stopped being a child... Actually, after Sharda left, I wasn't allowed to go anywhere, do anything.'

I was relieved to hear her talk. Obviously the sight of the books, something from her house, had opened up a dam of memories.

'I saw Binny on TV this morning.'

For the first time since I had met her, she looked at me eagerly. 'Really? Has she had her daughter?'

'Not as yet, but how do you know she's going to have a daughter?'

Durga was staring at the floor again; she had not heard my question.

'Daughters are terrible trouble, you must tell Binny to be careful. Do you know Manubhai is from Bihar? He got some Bihari labour to work on the farm. He also got his own daughters to the farm and then...' She stopped abruptly. 'Ask him what he did with them.'

After that, she would not say anything.

I wondered if I could get her to speak any more.

'Binny said to ask you about Rahul.'

She stared at the floor.

'Durga? Can you tell me about Rahul?'

The interview had ground to a halt. I picked up the books and returned them to my jhola.

Oddly enough, as she got up to leave, I thought I had made a breakthrough of some kind, but I did not quite know what it was. Maybe I needed to get back to the house. But before that, I thought I must also get hold of a Gurmukhi primer and perhaps fix to meet Durga's tutor. I still needed to talk to someone who had spent time with her before that terrible night.

I settled down finally at the guesthouse with a glass of cold beer, a primer and the papers. Lighting a cigarette, I spread them out in front of me, and read through the alphabets so I could recognize them. I wrote them down a few times so that they became familiar to me, once again. Then I turned the pages I had found at Company Bagh; they seemed to have been torn out of a lined notebook. The writing was very elaborate, as twisted as the one I had seen earlier, on the textbook. This was Sharda's writing then, not Durga's. Each page had been given a title. Perhaps they were part of a school project. My eye was caught by a curious scribbled sentence in the margin. Luckily, I could, slowly and painfully, read this. Sharda was agreeing to meet someone at 5 p.m.

I wondered if this could be one of the boyfriends mentioned by Amrinder's daughter. Or was it a note for the tutor? I remembered that Ramnath had said there was a married tutor who used to teach the two girls. I did not know if there were male teachers at St Mary's, but I needed to check.

I vowed to myself that I would hand over these papers to Ramnath (likewise the photograph), but only after deciphering them. If I was lucky, they would reveal to me the mystery behind Sharda's disappearance.

The telephone extension rang in my room. This time it was my friend Amarjit, asking if I was comfortable. Perhaps I was becoming paranoid, or was there a coolness in his tone? I had hardly seen him since I arrived, and yet I remembered a time when he couldn't live without me. All those motorcycle rides and secret meetings, such a long time back—perhaps he had forgotten them even sooner than I had. Not that I wanted to revive the memory, but a little friendliness at this moment would have helped.

He was waiting to hear whether I had made any progress. I told him that I had finally managed to get Durga to talk a little, and that it was very odd that she said all the photographs of her and her sister had been destroyed by the servants.

'She has an overactive imagination. I am sure the house has not been touched after the incident, except for the usual cleaning up,' Amarjit replied, his voice still formal. 'Ramnath has not allowed anyone to change anything in the house, because it is all part of the evidence for the murders. But do try to get her to tell you something, the press is really breathing down my neck about the investigation. I don't want to rush into anything. You see, her parents were such good friends, I want to make sure that she has a good chance of a defence... It would be great if you discovered that someone else did it and made her the scapegoat.'

Was that a hint to me? Was I supposed to concoct some evidence and give it to him so he could close the case and let her go? Did he, too, suspect as I did that she was being framed?

To binnyatwal@gmail.com

Hi hope all is well... must call you, do send me your phone number and when is a good time to call. Though of course I know right now you must be very caught up with the baby's birth. Durga is very sure that its going to be a girl! And that you'll call her Mandakini or Mandy!

She couldn't tell me anything about Rahul. Is he a boyfriend?

Take care, Simran.

PS: I think I should also change my name to Simi.

To simransingh@hotmail.com

Hi just the last few days now. Well, we always knew it would be a girl. They made me have an ultrasound. My pa-in-law took me. Durga was always on my side—she's my angel. Rahul is her adopted brother. Her mum adopted him 4 yrs back. I've said too much I think. Feeling very emotional today. Remembering my angel. Look after her. Bye for now. B

FIVE

13/9/07

Sometimes I think I could live like this forever. In limbo. I speak only when spoken to. Eat when food is placed before me. Drag myself around since the weight of my body has become unbearable. After all, what is the difference between being here and outside? I could go to school, I suppose, but learn what? Some of the girls in school like to talk about doing things and joining a profession, but I know all those are pipe dreams; ultimately, they will all get married, and then have children and be forced to stay at home (or go to the club every night, like my mother used to till she found religion might help her have a baby boy). But basically, do whatever the Darling Husband says. This is what my mother told Sharda and me, that we should stop feeling sorry for ourselves—because that is what happened to all girls. Not just us. And then we Would Grow To Like It.

I know that I am smarter and more clever than the other girls in my class, but I cannot demonstrate any of it because I must never attract any attention to myself. That is what he says. Be quiet and reasonable, don't show your temper. Don't ever get angry in public. *I still remember when he first started talking to me. I used to do my work at a separate table and he would supervise my sister. Then occasionally he would come across and look at my work and change it here and there. I liked his way of listening to me. No one else, except my sister, ever listened to me, and so this was very unusual. I would read the newspapers and books every day, just so I could say something to him, it didn't matter what. Even if I told him the astronauts had landed on Venus, despite the 500 degree celsius temperature, he would have listened to me and probably encouraged me to tell him more about it. He enjoyed all my little inventions, which became more and more preposterous as the days went by. It happens when you lead a reclusive life. You make up things all the time. I wonder now if I made him up, too. If I was so desperate for love, could I have just made it all up? Anything is possible. Perhaps I am mad, schizophrenic. They say it runs in families. I know that is what they are hoping for. Waiting for me to crack. Perhaps I will oblige them after all.*

I don't know when it was that I started playing games with him just like I did with my sister. When she wasn't in the room, I began to hold his hand. I began to understand why Sharda liked it so much, because I liked it too. It made me study harder. As soon as the lessons were over, he would listen to what I had to say and then hold me very tight. No one had ever held me tight, except Sharda, so I felt very nice all over. He told me not to speak about it, but he needn't have. Not after what happened to her.

In our Bhoot Bangla, there were secrets upon secrets. Things we all knew and never spoke about. Especially after Sharda left, and then Manubhai brought his two daughters to stay in the servants' rooms near the garden. Those rooms were next to my brothers' bedrooms, and I knew now why Amla used to say girls are nothing but trouble—which is why my father adopted Jitu, his own brother's son.

I always tried my hardest not to give anyone any trouble.

That was the biggest problem I think.

I have to say I was shocked when Binny told me about the sex-detection test in her email. I wonder if she knew it was illegal and that, for a well-connected family like the Atwals who knew the police officials intimately, rather dangerous. I was quite sure that the doctor's appointment would have been a special favour, secretly arranged. But, of course, they themselves owned some nursing homes. Was this another twisted skein in the complicated tapestry of Durga's life? No wonder her father had given away all that money in charity to the local hospitals.

Right now, there was little point even talking about this new information. It would not help to move the case forward and would only give the press some more sensational headlines. They had already put a picture of me in the local papers, confidently stating that I was a private detective hired by Durga's UK-based sister-in-law. Someone may have seen my emails to her; I had taken a print-out of them. After all, nothing could be secret in a police guesthouse. My only regret was that had I known I had such a glamorous role, I would have at least dressed the part in a trench coat and oversized dark glasses.

Thanks to this recent discovery of my 'real' purpose in Jullundur, there were two messages from TV channels who wanted to talk to me, as well as one from a newspaper journalist. Even the usually dour guesthouse manager looked impressed as he handed me the messages. I wondered if he was behind the rumours swirling around the streets of Jullundur. How much had he been paid to tell them this completely concocted story? I had already been tipped by him that the remand house warden was ready to give me 'information' about Durga if I wanted it. Just name the price.

'From Aaj Tak channel, saar,' said the manager. For some unknown reason, he could only call me saar. It had completely escaped his powers of observation that I was female. No wonder he was an efficient informer for the police force.

I told him that I did not want to be disturbed by anyone and sat down at my desk in the room, to try and understand the 'case' once again. Knowing that Durga was computer-literate, I logged onto the web and downloaded information on other well-known cases involving children. The internet may be one of my tools for investigation but for others, especially children, who are imitative by nature, it has a peculiar fascination.

Let me tell you, the fastest route to a long lasting depression is to try to understand why children get criminalized. Nothing is clandestine in this world any more and every incomprehensible crime is recorded, not just in words, but even videos you might stumble upon accidentally. I avoided the clips and went straight to the text, reading of recent cases in which children were the attackers. Even after so many years of working with juvenile crime, I am still taken aback by the desire for revenge and the uncontrollable rage that children can suffer from. If only, at that time, they had found someone to confide in, or if someone had counselled them: my ever-present wish and my most confounded hope!

The most recent brutal cases which came up on my screen were all again from the UK. Brian Blackwell, supposedly a brilliant student with three A levels, had taken his girlfriend to America for a shopping spree after he had knifed his parents because they had stopped him from meeting her. The peculiar thing was that, when he stabbed his father and his mother, the knife slipped in and out so easily that he did not think they were actually dead. So, according to him, he felt no remorse when he left his parents dying and bleeding on the floor. Brian was the only son and they had been loving parents. So what had gone wrong?

I wondered if we underestimated the impact of violence because television and other media used it so predominantly. Was the surfeit of blood-soaked cinematic brutality responsible for the lack of empathy for the victim? I looked at Brian's photograph. Did he remind me of Durga? They were separated by thousands of miles, yet joined by an anger and passion that purportedly pushed them to wipe out the very people who provided them succour and safe haven.

Of course, if parents could kill children and the newspapers were especially full of stories of men who raped and murdered their young daughters, why should the reverse not be true?

If parents could succumb to such cruelty, then children were easy enough to manipulate and exploit, even if there was no sustained provocation. From my experience in the Delhi jails, I knew that this happened quite often if a child from a disturbed background met someone they admired and fell under their spell: a mentor, or a cult figure with whom they could identify. Someone whom they idolized and who could easily groom them for any sort of crime, even murder.

The internet had transfomed even this process. The mentor could be physically out of reach and still affect children 'indirectly'. It could be a football player, a cricketer, a film star, a model, that is, people they never met or interacted with but whose wisdom they received through their games, films, music, photographs or media interviews.

There had been far too many cases recently, of adolescents receiving unintended messages from these mentors and harming themselves or others in some mistaken notion that they were being 'guided'. I had just worked with one child who thought he had to follow the mafia-type antics of film heroes. The 'messages' he received had only left him with a broken jaw, several disjointed ribs and a suspended conviction.

Could Durga have been exposed to any of these negative influences? Could there have been a role model or mentor either close by or far away, or a boyfriend or lover, who could have forced her to behave in a certain way? Or was this murder planned on the internet? I was sure the police had looked at the hard disc of her computer at her home—I made a note to ask Amarjit.

So far, I had not met anyone who was close to Durga. So was she the classic alienated, isolated person? I had no idea as yet of her relationships with her sister or brothers, or indeed her parents. Obviously, I was now reaching a point where I had to ask her, or someone who knew her, about her sister's story, her parents, the adopted son Rahul. The house on Company Bagh had been an enigma and now its residents were turning out to be equally incomprehensible. Every time I thought I was close to understanding Durga, she seemed to slip further and further away.

I felt I was standing in a hall of mirrors, in which I could see my reflection as a reflection of a reflection. And the last reflection, at the very end, was not of me, but of Durga. It was so tiny that it would take me a million years to reach there.

It was too early for a drink, so I smoked a cigarette instead. I took a deep breath, inhaling the smoke and holding it for a few seconds, forcing it deep into my lungs and urging myself to relax. Hoping for the best, I called up Amarjit's office to get the address of Durga's tutor, Harpreet Singh. As soon as I could get ready, studiously avoiding the inviting vibes I was getting from the pile of beer and whisky bottles, I took a rickshaw down to his house.

The route was circuitous. After braving several false leads and one-way traffic zones into which my rickshawallah waded with admirable insouciance, usually in the direction opposite to which the traffic was flowing, we finally found the house quite by accident, inside a narrow gali in the market. It sat above a tiny sweetshop and a dhaba which proclaimed under a colourful picture of a strutting rooster, 'Meet Me Anywhere But Eat Me Here', from which I gathered that its tandoori chicken was 'World Phamous'. The tiny doorway which nearly hid the steep concrete staircase leading up to the house was just wide enough for me to squeeze my way up, and I am not particularly large.

Obviously, Harpreet had not yet discovered the joys of teaching English to American students on the internet so that he could quickly earn millions of dollars and move to a posh bungalow.

A young girl opened the iron grille door and welcomed me inside. I was obviously too old to be a student, so she asked me if I had come to meet her mother. I shook my head and asked where her father was.

The girl was dressed severely in a traditional well-starched salwar kameez. She must have been around ten years old. She had two long plaits that flowed like brown waterfalls intertwined with blue ribbons over each shoulder. She said she would call her father who, it seemed, had gone down the road to teach someone.

I sat in the tiny courtyard around which most of the older homes are built—they are lungs for the whole house, providing the ventilation for the close, dark rooms which lead off from it. I could smell food being cooked in the kitchen but so far, no one apart from the little girl had come out. The curtain in the kitchen shifted a bit, and a woman emerged. I say woman, because she was dressed like one. She was completely disfigured, her wrinkled skin entirely covered with scars. Despite that, her dark eyes were quiet and friendly, glowing in a face from which her patchy hair had been roughly pulled back.

Without speaking, she handed me a glass of water and went inside again. I felt my breath grow hot and my palms became sweaty. What had happened to her? I was no stranger to these sights, encountering them usually in the hospitals where I went to record evidence of dowry victims, or young girls who had been attacked by acid thrown by jilted lovers. Looking around the room, I saw on the wall the portrait of a fair, pretty young girl, with a red and gold duppatta around her head. Was that her?

When Harpreet Singh entered the room, I was stunned

into a different kind of silence. This was a beautiful man. He had deep green eyes, dark wavy hair slightly longer than normal, and a gentle, peaceful expression.

'I am sorry to keep you waiting,' he said, and his Punjabi was as soft and polite as his expression. 'I was with a student. The exams are getting everyone into a frenzy. Has my wife given you something to drink? What would you like, some nimbupani, or tea?'

I stuttered as I asked for nimbupani. I was completely taken aback at the contrast between Harpreet and his wife. I suppose I had not expected to see someone like him. My own childhood experience of tutors was of grey, indeterminate creatures who were forced upon you by anxious parents. They came and went without leaving any impression, except the constant eye on the clock and the rigidity of their lessons. Most of the time I would try and hide under the bed, or get a stomach ache when I heard the cycle bell outside the door. With the cruelty of childhood, I had no time to think about whether they needed the job or not—I was only concerned about how to get them to shorten the lesson. The tutors I had for maths and Hindi had yellow teeth and bad breath. The only way I could escape them was to improve my own grades—and so I did. I never saw them again.

As he watched me calmly from his chair, I tried to imagine Harpreet and Durga in a closed room, and the picture disturbed me.

Something about his confident manner forced me to look away. He gazed at me as an equal and it was disquieting—since he was supposed to be only a highly forgettable, poor and humble teacher who did not earn more than a few thousand rupees a month. My mother often spent that much on getting her hair styled. For some reason, I was very conscious about my misplaced sense of superiority.

There was no disprespect in his gaze but he was not being obsequious either. He intrigued me and I suspected that he could sense my growing confusion. I struggled to find the right words to begin.

'I—I think you know why I'm here?'

'I read about you in the papers. You've come from Delhi to help with Durga's case.'

He was smiling quizzically.

I knew what he was thinking. He was not as dismissive as Ramnath but still curious about why someone like me would bother to get involved in a criminal case. I decided to make a joke about it. Keep it light and superficial—fit in with the image.

'The information in the papers is completely wrong. I am not a detective! Only a social worker. Amarjit and I were in college together, so he mistakenly thinks I can help out in some way. I have to say I am stumped, though. I haven't made much progress with Durga since she hardly talks to me... which is why I'm here.'

The effect of the green eyes was mesmerizing. I was talking too much, too fast and not giving him a chance to respond. I took a deep breath and bit my tongue. He continued to smile as one smiles at a failing student. *Don't worry, I know you can do it*. In a peculiar fashion, he made me feel rather small and insignificant. Then his amused look gave way to one of sadness.

'Durga has never been known for her conversation. She's quiet... but she feels things very deeply. This is a very hurt child, you know,' he said slowly and thoughtfully.

That was the first indicative statement I had heard from anyone so far. I was still looking at him, carefully absorbing his words, when his wife came out and served us nimbupani.

'Sit down, Sudha.' He looked at me again. 'Do you know why Sudha is like this? She was burnt in her first marriage because she brought insufficient dowry. Sudha, Durga... we certainly know how to treat our women properly. That child... should not be in jail.'

I saw the anger settle on his face. So he had married Sudha despite her scars and burnt condition. Should I allow myself to be impressed? Or suspicious? Was he too good to be true? I desperately wanted to believe him because in the world I came from, men like this simply didn't exist. And yet, warning bells louder than the traffic horns outside were ringing in my ears. I remembered Durga's face. Imagined her sitting with this man, studying. If he had this effect on a cynical bitch like me, who hated chocolate-box heroes, what would happen to a young girl? Why did her family, which was so conservative, choose him as a tutor? It didn't make sense. Something was wrong somewhere.

'I don't mean that she is too young for jail or anything like that, especially if she really did kill someone, which incidentally I don't believe,' he continued seriously, looking at me with just the right measure of compassion. 'I just think that these families who treat their women so badly deserve what comes to them. Durga is innocent. That's what you came to ask me, isn't it?'

'Actually...' Damn it, I was still stuttering like a five-year-old. This man was far too good-looking, and there was something about him that grabbed my attention, or perhaps something a little lower down in my anatomy. I had not felt this strange attraction towards anyone for a long time. I felt my face flush.

'I... I came to ask you to explain some of the family background. Not too many people here seem to know much about them—just generalities... rich family, parents very religious and so on. But there are so many things I don't know. For instance, did Durga love her parents, was she close to them?'

Harpreet leaned forward. His expression became even more intense. 'Is that a serious question? This is a fourteen-year-old child. Strictly brought up. Her life was spent between home and school. Of course she loved her parents. But did they love her? That's what you will have to find out when you finally speak to her.'

'Did you teach her regularly?'

'About twice a week. But I haven't been there in years. I was mainly her sister's tutor.'

He sat back as I digested that piece of information.

'And what happened to the sister?'

'Don't tell me Amarjit hasn't told you? Or what about his great friend, Ramnath? They all know. They visited Santji all the time—for every festival, on every occasion. They were there when Sharda...' He stopped suddenly, mid-sentence.

'I'm sorry, I don't know what any of this means. Are you saying they know where Sharda is?'

'That's right.'

'Where did she go?'

Harpreet was quiet once again. He looked at Sudha, who shook her head, ever so slightly. What was going on? I was beginning to feel more and more baffled. Maybe he was being extra cautious about what he said, since his wife was here too.

'I would tell you, but there is no point. It won't help Durga. And I don't think it will help you either. In this part of the world, the less you know, the better it is. In any case, let the police do their job, it's not your job to investigate.'

'All right... one last question... I got an email from Binny, Durga's sister-in-law in Southall. She mentioned someone called Rahul. Do you know anything about him?'

Harpreet got up abruptly and turned away to go through some books on a nearby shelf.

'Rahul came to the house in Company Bagh after I had stopped working there,' he said very carefully. 'Let me see if I can find any of Durga's books here. She wrote some short stories once, mostly fairy-tales with rather unhappy endings... perhaps I can send a book to her as well. She loves to read.'

I took out the Gurmukhi books and put the book he gave me inside my jhola.

'Do these look familiar?'

Harpreet slowly took the books out of my hand, and for a minute I thought I saw tears in his eyes.

'These are all Sharda's books. Where did you get them?'

'From the house.'

'The house? But...'

Sudha got up.

'I'm sorry, please excuse me, I have to make dinner.'

'Do you want to keep the books?'

Something I did not understand made me say that to Harpreet. Something in his eyes, the sorrow on his face. The droop of that perfectly shaped mouth. We were alone in the room now, and I felt his presence acutely. I was trying to remain dispassionate, but an odd affinity drew me towards him. Like me, he was fighting against injustice, but his reticence made it difficult for me to say anything more. It would have been too presumptuous.

At my words, he seemed momentarily transformed into a young boy.

'If I may. Just for a few days.'

'Sure... While you go through them, if there is anything that can help Durga, will you please let me know? Anything that would make her open up.'

I put every bit of my desperation into my voice. For god's sake, someone had to tell me something. I was in a complete fog right now.

'Sure I will.' He stopped to flip through the pages of the books in his hand. 'It's a strange thing to say... but it may give you some clue. Do you know what sometimes happens with women who are... inconvenient?'

'You mean like missing girl children? The ones who are killed at birth?'

'Yes, and later. You've seen my wife? Well, she survived. There are some who don't survive. Durga decided that she was going to survive. But others may not want her to. That's all I can tell you.'

I realized from his tone that the meeting was over. He sat down again with Sharda's books held to him, close like a shield.

I really hope I'll see you again. The words appeared in my mind unbidden. I stopped myself just in time before I said them out loud.

Mumbling a goodbye, I left through the narrow staircase, rushing as though the exit at the bottom would collapse before I reached. I was suffocated and breathless once again when I came down to the rickshaw. As I struggled for breath, the rickshawallah looked at me questioningly. No doubt he put it down to 'these modern shehri memsahibs' and their highly strung delicate nerves.

I cannot explain even now the sense of foreboding that overcame me. Was Durga meant to get out of this alive? Suddenly, I began to doubt the intentions of my dear college friend. Had Amarjit really brought me here to conduct some kind of grand cover-up? And even more worryingly, where was Durga's sister? This was obviously an even more complex story than I had imagined.

To <u>simransingh@hotmail.com</u>

Hi sorry u had such a terrible time with Harpreet. I wish I could tell u more, but as I said I never met him. Durga trusted him, tho. Called him Harpreetsir. But he is right, the less you know the better it is. I can only give u one hint, and pls delete this email as soon as u get it—or if u call me I'll tell u on the phone. Its to do with Rahul, but its such a terrible thing to tell. Call me tomorrow, but not from yr mobile phone. Always remember, they are trying to get a confession. Whatever else they may tell u.

Be v v careful—B

SIX

14/9/07

*Life in the Bhoot Bangla was always going to be difficult,
after Sharda left. I don't know why they had to pretend that
she had disappeared. They always knew where she was—and
they didn't know what to do about it. You see, they had
brought her up to go away with a dulha who would come in
a baraat. There were going to be many ceremonies, like when
the next-door girl got married. There would be the sangeet
and the mehndi and the vatna and the lavanh phere, and of
course, keeping with our status there would be lots of clothes
and jewellery—but Sharda didn't want any of that. The
moment she saw him, she was lost, and we could never find
her again. I used to worry because whenever she left at night,
I had to stay up and make sure that anyone coming into the
room would think she was in the bathroom, or I would pile up
pillows like they do in the movies and cover them with a sheet
and cuddle up, pretending it was her.*

*I could not fathom the change in her, it was so dramatic. In
front of everyone else, however, she was the same, so I don't
know how they found out. I think it was Jitu who got to know
first. Jitu had always adored Sharda. He used to call her Sita*

when he wanted to tease her, because he said as a little boy
he had discovered her buried in a pot in the ground. Actually
the dogs had found her, she was only a week old at the time,
but they thought she was a witch because she just wouldn't die.
At first they gave her opium and put her in a pot of milk and
twirled it around. Miraculously, the milk turned to butter and
the crying child still lived. The opium did not put her to sleep.
The midwife got worried and ran away, because she thought
Sharda had inverted feet, the sure sign of a witch.

Finally my grandmother picked up courage and instructed that
the wretched girl be buried in a clay pot in the earth at night.
Unfortunately for her, the dogs dug her out, and Jitu brought
her home, still crying for milk. He soaked milk in cotton wool
and fed her as he did the little puppies. And so Sharda became
Sita, because Sita, Ram's wife, was also found in the earth.
She became Jitu's special child.

And it was Jitu who found out where she went at night when
she grew up. He was uncontrollable.

How he changed towards her. It was to do with our high
caste and stature and the low caste and status of the man she
wanted to be with. It was to do with her being a witch and
a snake child and disobedient. It was to do with her being a
girl. It went on for days. They tried to do everything they had
done to her when she was born. The same Jitu who had saved
her life, now wanted to extinguish it. How is it that a girl can,
in sixteen years, go through exactly the same experiences twice
over. Except that they couldn't put her in a clay pot, she was
too big now.

༄

It was a bad morning. Mother called, as always complaining about her osteoporosis and arthritis. And wondering if she would still be alive by the time I decided to come home. (It had only been six days.) Not only that, she also went through the familiar routine of how much she would have enjoyed dying if she knew I was looked after, but how she couldn't even die happily and joyously because I had taken away the pleasure of even that by not hitching up with the first man who was crazy enough to propose to me... etc., etc.

I thought back to The Last Boyfriend. It seemed like another century. In fact, right now the world I was living in had less to do with tenderness and love, and more and more to do with brutality and deceit. To be quite honest, I was beginning to feel bewildered at the lack of compassion there was for Durga. Perhaps Harpreet did show some, but with his determined rectitude, he wasn't able to help me understand the situation, either. Unless someone told me which way to go, she would be abandoned. Even by me. How long could I stay here and try and ferret out the truth so that I could help her? I knew that Amarjit was getting increasingly impatient. It was a week already and I had nothing much to say about her condition. He had managed to buy her some time but it was, after all, three months and six days since that dreadful night. Yet, it was far too soon for Durga to come to terms with the enormity of what she had experienced.

I wished I could take her out for a walk, a movie, a few normal evenings, so that she could begin to trust me. Spend some time outside the remand home, but I knew it was impossible.

Thankfully, I was able to fix a phone conversation with Binny. It seemed a forlorn hope, but it was the only chance

I had of excavating a little bit of truth from the pile of misinformation everyone seemed to be feeding me. I had been especially startled by Harpreet's warning that Amarjit had something to do with Sharda's disappearance, that he knew more than he cared to reveal. I was equally worried about Binny wanting me to talk without being overheard, and that she thought my mobile phone and the guesthouse computers were both unsafe. Who could be interested in my mundane existence? And more importantly, what kind of confession were they after? Did they think I would, after all, trap the young girl, even though Amarjit had assured me he wanted to see her acquitted of all charges?

Moving like an old woman, I got out of bed and dragged myself in for a bath. It didn't help that the electricity had gone again, and the inverter made the fan move so slowly that each revolution barely disturbed the gigantic molecules of heat. My hangover from last night's serious effort at diminishing Punjab's liquor stock sat on my head like a demon. I knew that one must never drink alone. It was one way of becoming an alcoholic. But I no longer cared. If only I could resolve this case and get home. I wanted to start a new life, somewhere very far from Jullundur.

Groaning inwardly, I made the bumpy ride to the jail. It was about time to have a serious chat with Ramnath if he was back from Amritsar. Perhaps my mother was right (all mothers are eventually proven right) and I was taking this 'damn case' too seriously. I should just bung in a report, give my suggestions and run away. This had nothing to do with me, it was far too murky, and I could spend the rest of my life trying to find out where Sharda was. I didn't even know if finding her was essential to Durga's well-being. If everyone felt that it was safer for me to not know too much, why was I trying to move heaven and earth (and certainly both heaven and earth seemed to be moving rather too much right now) to rescue a teenager who refused to talk to me?

Just as I walked in through the fortress-like front gate, I found a crowd of women constables herding some Bengali women into a room. I knew they were Bengali because of the way they were dressed and also because one or two of them were very agitated and were loudly protesting at the treatment meted out to them. There was an obvious communication gap between them and the Punjabi cadres around them, who were in turn laughing or getting annoyed at the high-pitched racket. The way they were arguing, it seemed they were in a bazaar and bargaining for their freedom with whatever they had. The implication, unfortunately, was obvious.

There had been quite a few cases recently of women being bought for a few thousand rupees in Murshidabad and then brought into Punjab to service the farmers and other men. According to some NGOs working with sex workers, they were usually lured in by pimps who professed to love them, but when they arrived they were literally sold into slavery.

Ramnath stood to one side, talking quietly to one of the women inspectors and observing the new arrivals. So he was back from Amritsar, sadly for me. What was it about this man that I found so annoying, apart from the fact that his wife was still one of my least favourite people? I had to struggle to be civil to him. I pasted a pleasant expression firmly on my unyielding face and walked upto him.

'Hi. Did you see the Bengali brides?' Once again, there was the familiar mocking tone reminding me that I was very close to the edge, but getting angry would solve nothing. My head was still pounding from last night's drinking.

'Where did you find them?'

'Rounded them up in Mansa district. Can you imagine? We thought it was the men who were pimps. Lady, were we wrong! This bloody business is being conducted wholesale by a Bengali dame! She was bought in Murshidabad and sold to a farmer about twenty years back. And do you know, she thought it was a great dhanda. Got herself a farm with the profits. She's bought all these women, and she's going to sell them. Wow. What a sisterhood.'

While he chuckled and made his irritatingly arrogant and hopefully untrue observations, I looked at the young girls; most of them were tired and filthy. Their clothes were torn and stained. One of them, not more than sixteen, was sobbing into her saree. What was her fault? Why was she here at all? Recently there had been a flash flood in Bangladesh and refugees had sought survival in India. Who knew if these girls had found themselves without any option than to come here? There were no passports or voter ID cards in the darkness where they lived.

'That one there—she's the ring leader.'

My eyes were drawn to her. Dark haired, dark eyed, she stood, arms akimbo, chewing paan. Her curly hair was open, Aishwarya Rai style, and flowed down her back. She was better dressed than the rest, with her gold nose ring and green and gold net saree. She did not seem overwhelmed by the surroundings. How many times had she been here before?

'What will you do with them?'

'I wish I could send them back where they came from. But this is immoral trafficking, ma'am. We'll have to record the cases, put down the details. Most of them don't even know their parents' names. And they're all doped, you know. They have to be, otherwise when they find out they're going to be raped, most of them run away. So we have to wait till the effects of the drugs wear off.'

I wasn't sure I wanted to agree with anything Ramnath said, but that could explain why some of them were so quiet, while a few seemed terribly agitated. There were about eight of them.

The dark 'ring leader' suddenly shouted towards us, 'Aii, sahib. What's up? These girls are all supposed to be getting married. Why are we here? I've got marriage proposals for all of them. The big wedding—all together—is next week. Why don't you come for it? '

Ramnath laughed out loud, and shouted back, 'Why don't you tell the truth?'

'Ram kasam, sahib. It is the truth. These girls all have bridegrooms. I showed their pictures and then after they were selected, I brought them down.'

The woman's Punjabi had a strong Bengali intonation. I had never heard this strange mix before. Fascinating.

'You mean, you won't earn any money from them?'

'*Chee, chee, chee,* what are you saying. These are all my sisters. Don't I want to see my sisters happy, in a new home? In Murshidabad, sahib, there is no work, and no money. No good boys. In Punjab—we get very good men. They look after us. My husband is also a very good man.'

I looked at Ramnath. 'You can't keep her here if she is a married woman, and has an alibi. Maybe she is getting them married.'

'I think a few days in the Nari Niketan will sort out the moral issues.'

Knowing how these remand homes were run, my dislike for Ramnath became even more acute. I abruptly turned around and walked into the room on the side, where Durga was waiting for me. She had also heard the uproar.

'Who are all those girls?' She was curious. It was a good sign that at last she was showing an interest in other people around her. The deliberately blank expression on her face had been replaced by a more animated one.

'Well, according to the woman who appears to be the oldest among them, they all came from Bengal to get married.'

'You believe that?'

'I... honestly don't know. I've read of such cases, but I need to find out more about these girls.'

'Are you trying to fool me? You think I don't know the truth?'

Her harsh tone startled me. The anger had returned to her face. I was embarrassed to be ticked off by a young girl.

'Why would I fool you? Look, we all know that there has been a lot of... trafficking in women, especially in Punjab. You're old enough to know that. And out here especially, I mean, in jail, you'll see a lot of these women. But I do really believe that they are the victims. They are being exploited and so really, it is the men who exploit them abuse them and rape them, who should be in here.'

'In that case, you'd have to put most of the men you have met recently behind bars. Do you know that? '

'I think you should be careful before you accuse anyone. But if you have any concrete evidence, you can tell me.'

She laughed. 'Evidence? My god. It happened every day. In front of me. In front of my mother. In front of Sharda. That house in Company Bagh. My own brothers. The so-called daughters that Manubhai brought. Where do you think they came from? And for what purpose? Why don't you ask him?'

The venom in her voice, the hatred on her face. I could never forget it. The childish lines of her face hardened into rage. Her eyes stared beyond me into the darkness of her home. What had she seen?

'And do you know why? Because, after all, they were boys and needed to have some fun. So, you know, we brought these girls in. One was just twelve years old. Oh, it was all right of course, they were just animals, to be used. I don't think anyone bothered about what would happen to them eventually. I think Manubhai had paid three thousand rupees for them. That's less than a Gucci handbag, isn't it? Or, at least, less than a good meal in a five-star hotel. Of course, it was very discreet in the beginning. The girls were sent to the farm. But once the drugs started coming in, then Jitu and Sanjay both became quite careless.'

'But your mother?'

'My mother? She would just sit and pray all day in her pooja room. Oh, lots of kirtans were held, from morning to night. People in the house constantly praying, distributing karha parshad by the kilos, while the boys lay stoned in the next room.'

'Drugs? How could drugs come into your home? I mean, Amarjit is there and...'

'I didn't talk to you so far, because I thought you were stupid. You really like Amarjit, don't you? I think you even believe he cares about me. Oh no. Not Amarjit. And certainly not Ramnath. Do you know, if I want drugs... they could reach me tomorrow. Right here in jail. Do you think

Ramnath asked for you to come here? No, he was forced. This case is too high profile. He wants to know...'

She took a sharp intake of breath and shut up. Her eyes were suddenly full of fear as they slid past me to the door, where Ramnath stood watching us. Durga cringed back visibly. I remembered the rape and the marks on her body. Men would be difficult for her to deal with anyway. But in that split second something passed between Durga and Ramnath. It was so potent that I could feel the strain in the air. Of course he knew her parents and had been a frequent visitor to their house. Was that why she was scared?

Even more worryingly, how much had he heard?

His voice, when he spoke, was part persuasive, part seductive. 'So how are you, my dear? Are they looking after you?'

Durga got to her feet and her hands were trembling as she held them in front of her, like a schoolgirl ready for recitation. It seemed a familiar scene, as though she had been instructed in what to say. But the words seemed stuck in her throat. Beads of sweat formed on her forehead, and she nodded slightly.

No, not elocution. She was preparing herself for punishment. Her fear seemed to please Ramnath. He examined her with the same interest with which a botanist would watch a specimen wriggling helplessly at the end of a pin. The experiment, whatever it was, was going well.

I quickly got up because it was obvious that Durga wasn't going to speak in front of him. Nor did I want her to. I had finally begun to see a glimmer of light. I wasn't going to extinguish it that easily. I gave Ramnath my most charming smile. To block her from his view, I came a little too close to him.

'Hey, I think those Bengali ladies created quite a sensation,' I said, trying to divert his attention.

'And how are things here? How is Durga?' He spoke about her as though she were absent. His carefully combed hair smelt of Brylcream. As I came still closer, I could smell his aftershave lotion. Brut, no doubt. Everything about him was sharp, fresh, ready for action.

'Well… a long way to go as yet. But perhaps I should let her go back now. She's looking tired. And oh yes, I got you something to read.' I handed Durga the book Harpreet had given me.

She opened the first page and her eyes lit up. She looked at me and I could see a grudging gratitude for the very first time. She left without another word, and without looking at Ramnath.

For a minute Ramnath looked uncertainly at me. I was standing far too close to him. If I moved my head a little, I could rest it on his shoulder. Perhaps he was waiting for me to make a move. He put out his hand and touched my bare arm. His fingers felt cold and clammy. Before he could say anything, I gave him what I hoped was a mysterious smile and gently releasing my arm, walked out feeling like I had just climbed out of a snake pit. My headache returned as the adrenalin drained out of my body.

Outside once more, I made my way to a pay phone in the midst of a crowded market with the fruit-seller shouting in one ear and the paanwallah in the other. The sunshine and normality of it all calmed me down. How could such disparate worlds exist side by side without one affecting the other irrevocably?

Looking around to confirm that I hadn't been followed

and that no one was showing undue interest in me, I dialled Binny's number and shut the booth door. International calls to Southall are the norm in this part of the world, so there was no curiosity at all from the pay phone owner who continued to make some complicated calculations in the large notebook in front of him. It looked like a horoscope. Oh, yes—I noticed from the advertisement in front of me that in his spare time he was also an astrologer. Perhaps he was the person who would finally crack the case for me!

Binny's voice, with that peculiar cockney accent, brought a rush of reassurance.

'Hi Binny. How are you?'

'You got me just in time. I go to the hospital later this evening. Baby time.'

'Lovely to talk to you. Now tell me. You've had me very worried.'

'Okay. I can only tell you everything very fast because my mother will be back to pick me up and I can't speak in front of her. If she comes back, I'll just have to put the phone down. This whole thing has really spooked them. If they think I'm still involved in some way, it will scare them even more.'

'Okay.'

'Rahul is… Sharda's son. She left ages ago. I never met her. But I do know that it was something to do with him. She wasn't married, you see. I think they had put her in an asylum. I'm not sure. You could never speak openly in that house. Durga and I had to meet in secret because her father was very suspicious about how much she would tell me. But for god's sake, don't let anyone know you know he is Sharda's son. They simply said that he was adopted.'

'How did he go away with you?'

'It was—oh, I don't remember every detail of how it happened—but I went for a check-up and let's just say I was very upset because of the way my in-laws behaved. I don't want to say any more because they are both dead, and these things are best forgotten. But I was scared. Durga suggested I tell everyone that I was going to Delhi to visit some relatives... with Rahul. Luckily, he had a passport and I left for the UK with him. We had planned a holiday with the family, so most of the paperwork was already done—friends in Delhi helped, too. However, I don't want anyone to talk about the fact that he is here with me. I've kept him out of the news totally because I hope I can legally adopt him at some stage.'

'It's a bit strange. The timing of your departure. Did you suspect anything, any danger to the family, any hint from anyone?'

'No, no, no. You have to believe me—I was totally shocked when I heard about the deaths. Listen. I have to hang up now. But my advice, from what I heard from Durga: speak to Harpreet, or even his wife. They know more than they say. I sent you a letter a few days back—look out for it. Bye.'

The firm click of the phone brought me back to the Jullundur bazaar. Why had the check-up upset her? Was the family angry about the fact that it was going to be a girl child? To me there was a more plausible reason for Binny's need to leave: the two minor Bihari girls, the sexual trysts. Had she, like Durga, been exposed to any of it? And the drugs?

I had known, of course, that marijuana and opium were still a big problem in Punjab. In earlier years, we could always blame it on terrorism. That was the time when unemployment and the lure of easy money and drugs tempted many young people to buy into the myth of Khalistan.

Everyone knew about the large poppy plantations in Afghanistan which were the source of endless amounts of heroin. Those days, through a circuitous route via Pakistan, it finally reached Punjab and was further sent out to hubs where it was used for recreation or to blunt sensibilities.

But terrorism had declined recently, or had it? As far as the drugs were concerned, the channels once opened never really shut down. And now Punjab reportedly had its own surreptitious indigenous poppy fields, as well as ganja plantations. So had I stumbled upon yet another cruel fact that had distorted life at the house in Company Bagh?

One thing was clear—Sharda was the important link in this story. I wondered if I could show the photograph I had found to Harpreet. Maybe he could tell me who the girl was.

Dear Simran

I don't know if I will be able to speak to u, but I am sending this letter to Harpreet so that he will meet u. U might need his help to understand what's going on. Even though I never met him, I know that he helped both Sharda and my poor angel. Also because I want to warn u to be very very careful—emails can be traced, especially from the guesthouse. Remember that Sharda vanished, and these things are quite common, Durga had always warned me, so don't take it lightly. As u will find out soon enough, nothing is what it seems to be.

When I came to Jullundur, let me tell u, everything was a total shock. I knew that my in-laws were rich and that they were very traditional. I had been told that I had to give up my Brit lifestyle and get used to the traditional ways. I did that. I started wearing sarees and long salwar kameezes and covering my head. I met my husband for the first time on my wedding day. I did everything to please them because my mother was very keen on the wedding. They were from our caste, our biradiri. Yet the house was full of secrets. The strangest part of the house was Rahul and Durga; Durga, because no one ever spoke to her. Her father was incredibly cruel to her. She was made to feel like a complete idiot.

Even if she did well in school, her mother would simply look at the reports and put them away. Never a word of appreciation. I think they were angry with her. Because she had been loyal to Sharda and not told them that she was having an affair.

And Rahul—they made a big fuss about him, even though, let me tell u, he was being brought up as a girl. I thought he was a girl when I came to the house because he was dressed in a frock and had long hair. Since he was too young to go to school, they could keep him that way. Apparently they wanted to prevent the evil eye from falling on him. So he was made to wear frocks and ribbons. Someone had done some black magic on the family. Honestly, in Southall I had heard of these things but never seen any of it. Every day the servants would point out something suspicious—especially Amla, she once came to my mother-in-law with a ball of hair. It was Ammiji's and so she went into her puja room for three days. The worst was a doll with its limbs torn off, which the dogs brought in. Everyone went into hysterics seeing that. It was very odd.

So he was never called Rahul, just Guddi. Guddi! It was only when I bathed him one day that I realized the truth!

Then, when I chatted with Durga, I found out that he was Sharda's son. I am in the process of adopting him legally now. Poor thing! I don't know where his mother is, and why she was kept away from everything. I always thought she was still somewhere in the house. A few times I suspected someone was shouting in the middle of the night. Sometimes I thought I heard a woman scream, but it is such a big house and what with the dogs barking and the noise of the traffic, it was difficult to tell where the noise came from. Or if it was there at all.

There were too many things about the Company Bagh house that bothered me. Though I am a widow, and have to bring up a young child on my own, I am not sorry that I came away. I am sure I would have died with the others if I had stayed on. I owe my life to Durga... and my baby's life as well. If she had not told me to leave, I would be dead like everyone else. My god, am I grateful to her!

How do we get her out of there? Is there any legal information I can provide from here? I am sure the British legal system will be more sympathetic. Besides, Durga is just a helpless teenager. The Indian cops are having an easy time. They have arrested her because they simply don't have any suspects, and she is the most convenient, the fall girl. Maybe we can find some loophole. If only we could get her out of the prison and somehow bring her here. Durga could have never done it; besides, she was so badly treated, poor thing.

Take care—Binny.

SEVEN

17/9/07

The first time I was really scared was when Sharda told me her periods had stopped. Up to that point I knew what to do; after that revelation, I had no clue. Even though I was just nine years old, I had already been told the implications. And she was sick all the time. I didn't quite know how it all happened, but I was happy for her. She was planning her wedding to him, and said she would run away very soon. We made plans about how she would study further and go to business college in America. She was so good at following the share market, we felt she could soon be a millionaire.

It was very important to be financially independent. We knew already that she would have a difficult time because he was very poor. So she would have to work as well. Those were a few, very few lovely days. She was so happy at the thought of being a mother. When she came back, each night we would snuggle under the bedcovers and I would press myself against her warm breasts. They were no longer my sole terrain, but at least I could find some comfort in their softness.

We never once imagined that she would get rid of the baby.

Oh no. It was important that she started her new life with something of her own. The baby gave her something to look forward to. But Jitu put an end to all her dreams. He came in one day and insisted that she had to leave with him. She hadn't been out of the house for nearly a week at the time. It was the last time I saw her. They stopped talking to me because I had betrayed the family.

My mother came into my room one evening and hit me till I felt the skin on my face turn red with pain. I was supposed to continue going to school, and I went even with those bruises. I told the Mother Superior, who wanted to know, that I had fallen down some steps. I was worried someone would call home and check. But no one at home was interested in me any more.

From Amla I learnt that Sharda was in an asylum in Amritsar. But that was all I learnt. One day, Rahul came home with Jitu. He was such a lovely child. My mother insisted on calling him Guddi. She would dress him up as a little girl and buy him dolls all the time.

It's funny, isn't it? When she had girls, she didn't want them and now that she had a real boy of her own, she was too scared to admit it to the world and wanted to pretend he was a girl. But somehow, none of it was funny.

It was around this time that my brothers started taking drugs and Manubhai brought in his 'daughters'. I spent all my time now with Rahul/Guddi. I knew he had something to do with Sharda but I didn't know, and still don't know, if he is actually Sharda's son, or just someone my mother brought in to lavish her love on. She had never cared for me anyway, and my brothers were now far too independent.

Besides, Ammi's love was too important to be wasted on me. Now she said that the older boys had let her down. Rahul was her only hope. But the world was not supposed to know who he really was. She had to hide him away somewhere safe. In case someone hurt him too.

I often wondered if that 'someone' was my father, her husband, Santji.

As the train pulled out of the filthy Jullundur station, with its broken staircases, dilapidated platforms and limbless beggars, I sat back with a sigh. I hadn't been here for so many years, I had actually forgotten the horror of it all. One had to dodge the pickpockets too, who normally nicked your money just as you were stepping into the train. It was a minefield of discomfort. And then there were the frequent announcements made in Swahili which came on after the train had left. So that before you realized they had mentioned your train, it had already rolled out of the station.

Of course, there was no certainty that you would actually reach your destination, as explosives on trains were a common feature. Never having encountered a real suicide bomber (i.e., people who got onto trains with explosives *inside* their bags), the railway police walked around the compartments putting little black stickers with numbers on your luggage. It was their simple belief that if you were able to identify your bags successfully and got a number on a black sticker, you would never blow the train up. This spectacular faith in numerology and the power of possession defied logic.

If it is any consolation, on an Indian train you could die of other causes too. Filthy bathrooms and greasy food, for example. But at least, here I was. Still breathing. Somewhat dented by recent events—but still alive.

I had met the manager of the guesthouse in the morning and told him I would be away for two days in Amritsar. I could see he was getting a little concerned about me. Reports of the empty beer bottles and piles of cigarette butts had no doubt begun to worry him. Well, he wasn't my father; I didn't owe him an explanation. But I knew that, sooner or later, the gossip about me would reach Amarjit and Ramnath, the two men who were in the midst of the investigation and, in a sense, my allies. I didn't actually care about their opinion, but I did wonder why I was not being invited to their homes, as good Punjabi hospitality demanded.

Could it be my determinedly adolescent behaviour, my inability to conform? Were they worried that their wives and children would be polluted by my presence? That was odd because one marriage, I knew, was already dysfunctional and the other one was built on pure ambition. The fact that I had been accused in the past of being responsible for Amarjit's increasing distance from his wife was no longer relevant. After all, we had all come to terms with it, each in his or her own way. Besides, I would have never been invited to Jullundur if that was still an unresolved issue. So there had to be some other reason why these two had decided to leave me rather severely alone.

Though I consoled myself that I wasn't really bothered by their disinterest in me, I *was* piqued. My ego was bruised. After all, compared to the average Jullundurite, I should have been the much more interesting, well-travelled outsider, an exciting addition to their dull evenings. The bohemian woman-about-town who went against the grain, the rebel about whom they could say accurately, 'We always knew she would come to no good.'

But obviously, nothing in my portfolio could overcome the fear of contamination. I was always the wild one, and therefore, slightly disreputable. Certainly not enticing enough to be placed near Swarovski crystal animals on a glass table. Perhaps my notoriety would shatter glass. To keep me out of their drawing rooms was obviously a safe bet for Ramnath and Amrinder.

But Amarjit? That was a surprise. Considering that I was doing him a favour, or let's say *another* favour in a long list, some of which he could hardly forget. I remembered a time when he wrote poems in my honour. How the mighty had fallen, even though the poems did not bear remembrance!

Yet, I have to say the benign neglect was a relief. I actually did not want to spend my time in schoolgirl gossip or rancour. There was a vast chasm between me and my old school and college chums. And I knew it. The sort of places I spent my time in had cut me off from their lives forever. While they wanted to talk about the latest Hollywood film or the sale in Harrods from their last trip abroad, I spoke about undertrials and the slow judicial system. We would probably have an argument if they tried to patronize me, a middle-aged, frustrated spinster, drowning her sorrows in drink and worrying about children who spent their lives in jail. Not even very pretty, any more. I looked at the window which reflected a thin, sharp featured face with large dark eyes, staring back at me morosely. I lifted my coffee cup to the grim reflection—'Cheers!'—and knocked it back.

In any case, I didn't think I had time to socialize. There were too many loose ends in this case.

I pulled out the files again from my briefcase, put on my spectacles and carefully went through the information on Sharda. It was very limited, and there wasn't even a photograph to help me. I took out the photograph of the girl on the bed from my jhola where I had hidden it. As advised by Binny, I had decided to be exceedingly cautious and carry all my files with me. After all, the Inspector General of Police in Haryana had been accused of molesting a very young woman a few years ago. Another senior officer in the police had recently been charged with murdering a reporter in Delhi, allegedly his mistress. None of this, or my own recent experience in Jullundur, inspired any confidence in my friend, Amarjit. Anything could happen, and no one could be trusted.

Could this picture of Sharda have been taken in the asylum? But it could also be a hospital bed. If Rahul was her son, it could even be a nursing home. The starkness of the girl's surroundings was mysterious. I had also just spotted what looked like the links of a chain on the side of the bed which bothered me enormously.

From experience I knew that even in the twenty-first century, mental health hospitals in India were still largely a dumping ground for the 'inconvenient' as Harpreet called them. Many women were locked up simply because they were not wanted by their families, and minor incidents were blown into catastrophic events. A large proportion of women in these hospitals were well into their middle age and often had husbands or families who found them difficult to live with— too aggressive or argumentative. Sometimes there were issues of inheritance, or the husband wanted to get re-married. It was certainly a cheaper option than a divorce.

One brave survey had shown that we had less than three psychiatrists per million in India. It was a paltry and ineffectual figure—given the problems of poverty and social tension which were now beginning to surface. When forty per cent of the population did not have access to decent education, health or even nutrition, obviously there would be enormous mental problems. But there were few institutions where help was available. Did we even care that in most developed countries there were at least a hundred psychiatrists per million people? And it was doubtful whether the few we had were properly qualified.

I didn't know what I would find in the Amritsar mental health hospital, but on the train I read an interview with one of the previous directors. He had admitted that 'mentally ill patients were abused, beaten, chained, and tortured. They were forced to do hard labour and perform menial jobs of cleaning floors, washing bathrooms, toilets and soiled linen. They were also made to wash incontinent patients and perform other chores...' For all this, they were given electric shocks without anaesthesia. One staff member had been dismissed for brutally beating a woman patient. That was only five years ago, when Sharda must have been admitted there.

From what I could assume, and from all that had been told to me, her story followed a common enough pattern as she had also become 'inconvenient'. My conjecture was that her family had found out that she was having an affair and the only way to teach her a lesson was to make her 'disappear'. She had crossed the lakshman rekha. In a tradition-bound small town like Jullundur, sex outside marriage was taboo.

Only the tribal family elders could decide who a woman could marry and sleep with.

The train pulled up at the Amritsar station, and the compartment was soon swarming with red-clothed coolies. I pushed them and my overpowering depression away, struggling to reach the exit through the crowds of non-resident Indians and Golden Temple devotees. I found a taxi and asked the driver to take me to the paagalkhana, as it is still known around these parts. The mad house.

Built in the 1950s, the hospital services all the neighbouring states. It has only around three hundred beds for women. And patients come from Haryana, Punjab and Himachal Pradesh, a population of at least twenty-five million. So, like with everything else in the country, you have to struggle to get a place in the mad house. You can only get admitted on someone's sifarish. You have to know a VIP.

The hospital with its dismal red and grey structure was easy enough to find. After presenting my credentials, I made my way to the director's room. I did not have a prior appointment, so I was asked to wait till he was free. In the background I could hear some people exercising. The sound of their activity mingled with the steady drone of a TV announcer reading out the news. A few women in white sarees went in and out of the waiting room, and alongside me sat two anxious looking couples. One of them had a catatonic young man with them, who abruptly got up and began marching up and down. He paid us no attention, and after some time I stopped counting the number of times he sat down and got up. Certainly I did not hear any screams, or see uncontrolled patients running around, but I knew that the really serious cases would be somewhere deep inside the building, in wards and cells, where we could not hear them.

After fifteen minutes, when I was finally called in, I found that the director, Prakash Goel and I had previously met in Delhi at a conference on women and incarceration. It helped to open the conversation but at the same time it was apparent that he had just taken over and was still learning the ropes. I explained that I was helping with the Atwal multiple-murder case and was looking for records of Durga's sister.

'Sharda Atwal. Let me find out.'

He rang for the file and told me about the changes he was trying to make to the place. He came from a family of doctors settled in the UK, and he was still idealistic enough to believe that he could actually make a difference. Given my own cynical disillusionment, this was a pleasant change.

'I wish the families would get more involved. Some of these women should really go home, there is nothing some love and affection will not cure, so I am trying to see if I can set up a rehab home for them, outside this centre, something a little more soothing. Who knows who among them may actually recover?'

He gave the familiar argument that perhaps inclusion would be a good way to help them. If only they could be allowed to go home, and have regular medication and checks to help them lead normal lives. After the horrific accounts I had been reading, it was extremely reassuring to find someone who could sympathize with the inmates. Losing your mind was very unromantic, especially here, in an institution that was notorious for locking up criminals alongside the genuinely ill people, to give them an escape route from punishment. Prakash recounted the recent brutal death of a young girl, within the asylum, who had also probably been raped. It had happened just when he had taken over. But there were no records of where she had come from, or who her family was. So perhaps her death in this safe house was not very different than if she had been out on the street. Even more worryingly, he pointed out how very often, mentally challenged individuals were mistaken for being mentally ill. He was still trying to sort it all out. I could see the exhaustion behind his determinedly cheerful manner.

When the file arrived, I was pleasantly surprised once again. I was so used to a system in which paperwork mysteriously vanished all the time. It usually lessens the burden of work on the staff, when they can announce, 'File is lost, saar.'

Prakash opened Sharda's file and went through the pages. It was an impressively thick document. Again, very unusual for this part of the world.

'Is there a history of mental illness in the family?'

'Not that I know of.'

'Well, here there is a testimony by someone whom she attacked at home. Almost killed him, it seems. She was diagnosed with schizophrenia and severe depression. She was admitted here first in 2002, given some drugs to help her stabilize. A long list of these is attached. Then someone came to get her. Perhaps she had been raped previously? That's the accusation made by one of the family members, because she was pregnant. She was brought back after the child was born, and then... some more treatment and that's it.'

'That's it? What happened to her? What kind of treatment?'

'Oh, things to calm her down. The doses are quite high, so she must have been violent.'

'Electric shocks too?'

'I am afraid so. We don't do it any more.'

'I read that in the past it was done without anaesthesia and that most of the staff were untrained.'

'What can I say? All sorts of things happened here in those days.'

'Where did she go?'

'It seems the family came to take her away after a year or so.'

'Is there a picture of her?'

He showed me one in the file. It was of a painfully thin woman, with a scar across her forehead, and short cropped hair. Her mouth drooped on one side and her eyes were glazed over as she stared vacantly ahead. It was a look I had seen far too many times. I thought I could see a faint resemblance to Durga, but it was difficult to say.

Prakash was looking a little worried now.

'You say the sister is in judicial custody because they think she may have murdered the family? How many people?'

'Thirteen.'

'I know you are trying to help her but now that we know her sister had a history of mental illness, could it be possible that she is also perhaps a little unbalanced? '

I drew back sharply from the desk.

'She is a perfectly normal teenager. And let me tell you, most of the things written about Sharda are complete lies. This was a family dispute, she fell in love with someone and so they locked her up. It's not unusual, you know that surely.'

'Don't get so emotional, Simran. I don't want to upset you, but it is possible that this file actually tells the truth. And that her sister is capable of murder. This might sound very simplistic to you, but sometimes, in their more lucid moments, the people who are supposedly insane can control us. They push all the right buttons, make us feel guilty, and get away with all sorts of crimes. It's a very thin line, as you know. Try and remain objective. I know this is just a fourteen-year-old kid but I have seen people develop inhuman strength, mental and physical, if they are provoked enough. Murder would be very easy.'

His voice rang in my ears as I walked out. In my confusion, I thought that his secretary-cum-receptionist looked a little too knowledgeable as I walked past her desk. Why was she giving me such a strange smile? What information did she have? Before I could say anything, she went into Prakash's room. Beads of sweat covered my face. Had I made a complete fool of myself? Was I so easy to manipulate?

Just then, a line of women inmates walked past me. They were all quiet and bent over as though carrying some invisible weight on their backs. A few of them were thin and emaciated, like the girl in the photograph I had seen. I knew they were fed the minimum food and their blankets were stolen from them in winter. I knew they often arrived with lice in their hair and worms, yes, worms in their eyebrows, and how the staff refused to clean them up. I knew their identities and their last shred of dignity had been ripped from them. But what could I say, right now? Had I just made the biggest mistake of my life?

I walked into the sunshine. It was a blazing hot day. Even the birds sat quiet and parched in the shade. At least I knew that Sharda had been in the asylum. And I had learnt a little more of the family background. Taking a deep breath, I went back to ask the secretary for a copy of her photograph. I must keep my cool and remember that my first priority was to help Durga. None of this was going to be any good, if she too ended up in the paagalkhana like her sister. Was that what everyone was trying to force me to do? Recommend that she be locked up in here?

I had a moment of epiphany as I sat back in the train to Jullundur. Was Binny as innocent as she was trying to appear? Why hadn't it struck me that she had the most to gain if Durga was locked up—either in jail or perhaps even in the asylum? It made perfect sense for Binny to put her sister-in-law in the asylum—there was a large inheritance, wasn't there? It was uncanny and suspicious that she left right before the murders and that she escaped unscathed. And then she dropped hints and nudged me towards the asylum. All done with such competence.

My mobile phone rang. It was Harpreet. He had received a letter for me, from Binny. Talk of the devil. I arranged to meet him the next day. I listened to the sound of the train rattling along the platform and tried to relax.

To simransingh@hotmail.com

Dear simran, u'll be happy to know I had a baby girl last night. Please tell durga. She will be thrilled. Take care, Binny

Ps : The sender of this message is actually Binny's mother. My name is Santosh. I hope you don't mind my writing to you, but Binny wanted to let you know.

To <u>binnyatwal@gmail.com</u>

Dear Santosh,

Many thanks for the message. Congratulations and do tell Binny I'll convey the message to Durga. I hope she and the baby are doing well. Simran

EIGHT

Of course I missed her. They removed everything of hers from my room, her clothes, her books. It was like she had never existed. If anyone asked about her, they said that she was unwell, and away for some treatment. Honestly, for a while even I believed that. I knew about the baby of course, but couldn't ask because like a fool I thought it was a secret between her and me, and no one else would ever find out.

One day, I did think I saw her at the annexe, a small two-storey building behind the house. You could just about glimpse it from my room, through the trees. This was in the morning when I was getting ready for school. Or, at least, there was someone who looked like her—but she had very short hair and was very thin and so I wasn't sure. She was being taken inside by my father. And then Manubhai called the driver and I was taken away to school.

You may wonder why I never went to check the annexe. But there was a murder there some years ago and after that none of us liked to go there. The servants had told Sharda and me about the blood splattered on the wall. They said a terrorist

111

had been killed in an encounter. I suppose I was also scared of upsetting anyone. After she left, I was on tenterhooks all the time, the atmosphere in the house was suffocating. I didn't want to make things worse by stepping out of line. Till that time, I really thought if we all behaved as though nothing had happened, nothing would happen to her. Or to the baby.

Then, one day, my father sat down at dinner time and announced, 'It's going to be a boy.'

My mother looked at him and she almost smiled for the first time in many days. I was at the door, and they hadn't seen me. All my meals were given to me in my room. I was still being punished.

'Another six months.'

Then she saw me and got up to shut the door. I went back to my room.

So when Rahul arrived, a new born, tiny little motherless thing, I thought now she'll come home any day. But the servants whispered and gossiped. I overheard that she was 'possessed'. They had tried to get her exorcised. A baba had come from Hoshiarpur. She was seeing things and would scream for no reason, especially if my father came into the room. She had tried to run away. They had to lock her up again. They had no choice—*kudi kharaab ho gayee.*

The idea that a girl could get spoilt, like milk gets curdled, was a new concept for me. Maybe it was the heat. I didn't think she was bad, she had simply fallen in love and there seemed nothing wrong with that. Why couldn't my parents or my brother accept her the way she was? Despite their anger, I

still thought it was all wonderful. Every night I expected her
to climb in through the window and snuggle down with me,
with her familiar laugh. I opened the window wide every night
and prayed to all the gurus and the gods. I recited my Japji
regularly. I did whatever I was told to do.

But she never came back.

I hadn't slept most of the night. The information from the
asylum kept going through my mind. I also knew that I must
go across early in the morning to tell Durga that she was now
an aunt. It would cheer her up. I had begun to feel even more
responsible for her. And I was still worried that somehow my
going to the asylum had further endangered her. If no one
had yet made the link between Sharda's madness and Durga's
suspected violence, I did not want to be the one to suggest it.

As though to confirm my worst suspicions, Amarjit called
me early in the morning on the phone in my room. I had
switched my mobile phone off. I tried to save money whenever
I could, though it probably made very little difference because
when my mother called, the conversation could last several
hours. She could never understand why, despite having been
left a large fortune by my father, I never wanted to spend
it. My burden of guilt was unfathomable, since for her it
had always been easy come, easy go. Even when my father
finally 'went', thanks to long hours of work and the stress
of 'performing', standards had to be maintained. What was
money for, if not to be spent?

'So you were in Amritsar? Why didn't you tell me?'
Amarjit's voice was slightly aggrieved.

'How do you know?'

'Sweetheart, I'm supposed to be a policeman, remember? I have informants, people tell me things they think I need to know.'

'And what else?'

'Didn't you know her sister had been locked up there?'

'No one told me for sure. I wanted to check it out for myself.'

'You thought she may still be there? Did you look for her?'

'No, the director told me he had no idea where she was, that the family had taken her away. You must know where she went.'

'Why don't you ask our heroine? She may give you a better idea.'

'Amarjit, are you trying to say that she killed her sister or put her in the asylum? You are talking about a child, a fourteen-year-old child. From her reactions, I think Sharda may have been the one person Durga really cared for.'

'Well, I don't know either. You find out. Only... the media and my bosses want to know how long it's going to be before we announce the case details. I have told everyone she is still under medical supervision. What's your opinion, now?' Was it my imagination or was there a note of impatience in his voice?

'I've always believed her, that she is innocent, that she is a victim. I think her sister was a victim too. But let me talk to her. She still doesn't want to speak about what happened. Just give me a few more weeks.'

'Okay. I'll try to give you some more time, but remember, we'll have to come to some conclusion fairly soon. You know why I asked for you and not a professional psychiatrist. I genuinely want to save this girl. If I had brought in a psychiatrist, the press would have made the connection and that would have been the end of Durga's chance for freedom.'

I understood Amarjit was being unconventional. It was a big risk, but I still didn't trust him. He had known about Sharda all along and wanted it kept quiet. He had explained his own reasons and I could sympathize, but it was also peculiar that, so far, no one had traced Sharda to the asylum. No one was really bothered. And no one knew what had happened to her after that. How could someone vanish without a trace?

I put the phone down slowly, feeling a little better only when I remembered that Harpreet was also coming over this morning. I had been disturbed by our first meeting, yet the fact that he was taking the trouble to meet me had an old-fashioned chivalry to it, much needed in this part of the world. I felt especially vulnerable after Amarjit's brusque conversation. Perhaps, if I presented my softest side to him, Harpreet would give me a little more of the information he had withheld last time.

Whether it was merely to extract information by playing the femme fatale or because I remembered the devastating effect he had on me, I took out my least shabby saree, a bright yellow, and put my bindi on with extra care. I even took out my silver earrings and clipped them on. Normally I don't really notice men or bother about whether they appreciate me, yet, looking into the mirror I was pleased to see a slightly improved version of myself. I carefully patted down a few curls on my forehead. Made me look less severe. Perhaps I should wear bright colours more often—they suited my dark skin.

I put the photographs of Sharda into my cotton jhola. Just as I was stepping out of my room, I saw Harpreet enter the sitting room of the guesthouse. So far, I had successfully pushed the thought of him into the deepest recesses of my mind, where I hoped they would not bother me any more. But damn! The man seemed to have become even better looking within a week. Life was simply not fair. It wasn't just the way he looked, but the caring person he appeared to be. An idealistic man married to a disabled woman, with a poorly paid job when he could be earning much more. He had been worried about Durga, tearful over Sharda. To keep my distance from him, I had to remind myself he might be less altruistic than he appeared—but it was a tough mission.

I knew the consequences of being drawn to the wrong kind of man only too well. After all, The Last Boyfriend, a straight-talking, slightly dull human being whose main drawback was his Mummyji fixation, had not been entirely at fault. I knew I had pushed our relationship to the edge, and finally he just could not indulge me any more.

Perhaps I liked to live dangerously, but this addiction to risk was hopeless: I tried to conjure up my mother's anger and annoyance over my less than perfect behaviour.

'If he is involved in this murder in any way, it will only lead to heartbreak,' she would say, shaking her finger sternly at me. 'Besides, he is a married man.' Maybe I enjoy a challenge, I would argue back.

Right now, however, I tried to control my nervousness.

He handed me a letter from Binny, and I thanked him for coming. We sat down and I began reading the letter immediately.

Those green eyes seemed to see right through me, to my

confusion. This was not a man my doctor would recommend. Like my mother, I was now familiar with palpitations.

Even as I read the letter, I imagined us talking, sharing a meal, even holding hands. It was a crazy desire. Maybe the strain of the last few days was becoming too much for me.

We ordered coffee, and sipped it as I finished the letter.

'She says I could ask you more about her in-laws and Durga.'

He shrugged. 'I'll do my best.' He was careful not to allow any emotion into his voice. We could have been discussing the weather. I also tried to keep the longing I felt out of my eyes, my face, my voice.

I told him about my trip to Amritsar, but he remained impassive, looking away as I gave him the details. If I concentrated hard enough, I could keep the meeting formal, I told myself in the same tone that my mother might use.

Finally, I picked up courage. 'Do you know about Sharda's son?'

'Of course I do.'

'Did you meet him?'

'Never.'

'Will you meet him?'

'I'm not quite sure where he is now.'

'Harpreet,' I said as gently as I could. 'I know you have a wife and a daughter, so I really shouldn't ask you this, but…'

'I know what you want to ask me. But the thing is, it was a pact with the devil.'

I was taken aback. This was not the response I had expected. I was talking about his fondness for the two sisters, and he was saying something else. I lit a cigarette and offered him one as well. He refused and in my nervous state, I thought he may even have disapproved. Well, too late now.

'Who did you make the pact with?' I asked stupidly.

'Sharda's father,' he replied pityingly. Hang on, I wanted to say, as the floor seemed to heave up at me.

'You made a pact about Sharda?'

'That's right. I promised I would never see Rahul if they allowed me to meet Sharda. They agreed. I didn't know why till I met her.'

The ground shifted once again under me, as the real meaning of his words sank in. My own stupidity hit me like a runaway train. I groped for words, but for a few moments could find none. Waves of sickness washed over me.

He too fell silent and stared out, through the window. I thought the mask dropped from his face, and anger blazed in his eyes. He had looked away so that I could not see the true extent of his rage, but he wasn't quick enough. *He had loved her, perhaps he still did.*

'Why was that?'

'She was completely gone by then, those electric shocks, the beatings, had destroyed her completely. She was very ill. They sent me the address where I could find her. It was a village in Hoshiarpur, where she had been left with some baba, an exorcist, because they said she was possessed. I would never have recognized her. She used to be beautiful. Now she was all skin and bones, with no hair, and boils on her body from the malnutrition and the burns and the beatings. She had stopped eating and all the time, she would pick up small children and press them to her breasts, saying they were hers.

'The villagers thought she wanted to steal their children. Or she would scream for Durga and hit her head till it bled.

We couldn't stay there, so I came back for one day to arrange for a place so I could bring her back with me and… that's the last time I saw her.'

I took out the photograph of the girl on the bed.

He looked at it and carefully took it from me. He was silent for a long while.

'Where did you find this?'

'In the house. Do you have any idea where it was taken?'

He looked puzzled; it seemed he had never seen the photograph before.

'I don't know, maybe in the asylum?'

'So where is she now?' I asked, praying that he would say he did not know. Trying to keep my voice from shaking.

'Her family said they had given me all the information they had.'

'Someone knows where she is and cares. Because why does Amarjit still want to know where she is?'

'He hundred per cent knows where she is. In fact, Ramnath arranged for her to be taken to the asylum. He got her admitted so that no one would know about the child. Her father probably asked him to arrange something. Actually, he doesn't need to bother any more if she's dead or alive because she will never be a danger to him in her condition… She will never recover enough to give evidence against him or his friends at the asylum, if that's what he's worried about. It was systematic abuse. Criminals are deliberately admitted into the mental hospital just to save them from the gallows, and others are driven mad just to keep his contacts happy… like Sharda.'

'Do you have any proof? The director of the asylum is a friend of mine, perhaps there is something we can do?'

'If you make too much of a fuss… be careful they don't say Durga is crazy as well. The director is new and he has to survive too. If you live in a lake, you don't antagonize the crocodiles.'

'How much of this does Durga know?'

'She knows most of it… You can understand her anger. This is a sister she absolutely adored.'

'How were they able to do all this? Why didn't anyone say anything to save her or protest?'

Harpreet shrugged.

'It's a rich, respectable family. They run schools and orphanages. Ammiji would pray every day for six or seven hours at a time… Santji, as the father was called, was always funding charitable causes. There was plenty of money for everyone. For Amarjit, for Ramnath. The only problem was they just didn't want girls in the family, and if they had them, they had to follow a strict code of conduct. That, incidentally, is why Sharda survived. Her ultrasound at the asylum showed that she was going to have a son. It saved her life.'

I took out the photograph of her taken at the asylum. 'Is this her too?'

'That's how she looked when I last saw her.'

There was so much passion in his voice that I involuntarily put my hand over his. He was a surprising man. He caught my hand and gently pressed my fingers and I felt warmth rise within me. I knew he was angry and helpless, yet the way he looked at me now said something else.

It was a moment when everything seemed to go very still. There were only the two of us. Anything was possible in that split second.

As I withdrew my hand, his green eyes seemed to convey

his hurt. It was like being on a rollercoaster. I still did not have the guts to ask him if Rahul was his son. I felt awkward. In my own head it didn't matter, though my heart was saying something else. Despite my effort to appear cool and collected, my voice shook slightly as I spoke. I was still feeling sick.

'You're very brave. You took them on. They could have killed you, or perhaps had you put away.'

'Don't make me into a hero. Had I been braver, Sharda would still be with us.'

He had barely left, and I rushed to the bathroom sink to throw up. All that excitement, all the build up—only to find out that there was a very strong possibility that Amrinder and Ramnath may yet be correct. Why was it *always* so easy for me to fall for the wrong person?

As I left for the jail, I carried his words with me. I knew I should stay away from him. This man could complicate my life forever. Usually, at least when I was working, I managed a professional detatchment. But this time, everything was different, and the strength of my own involvement unnverved me.

It was probably the stress and loneliness of being in a small town that was getting to me. I remembered how, when I was growing up, you only needed to spend an evening alone with someone of the opposite sex to convince yourself you were in love with him. These encounters were so infrequent and rare in the conservative and more traditional backwaters, that hormones leapt at the slightest opportunity. It was why two perfect strangers could be married off to each other and be expected to fall in love overnight. It was only a chemical reaction—but it happened all the time in small towns. Believe me.

I pushed Harpreet out of my mind and thought determinedly of Sharda and her lost youth.

I knew that from now on I would scrutinize the face of every derelict homeless woman I saw on the streets. The women we avert our eyes from, the ones who sashay past in torn clothes and filthy matted hair, certain in their madness that no one could hurt them any more.

In the anteroom, Durga was waiting for me quietly.

'I have wonderful news for you. Mandakini was born last night!'

Durga's eyes filled with tears, but her face was radiant with joy.

'I don't know if you understand how important this is for me, for us.'

'I know... I also want to tell you that I went to the asylum. I know about Sharda. I think that's what you wanted. It is terrible... and all because she was going to have a baby. The poor, poor girl.'

She reached out suddenly and I hugged her. It was the first time she had touched me. But, strangely enough, she completely ignored what I had said about Sharda. It was as though she hadn't heard me.

'I am so happy about Mandakini. Tell Binny they lost and we won.'

'Who lost?'

She was speaking in riddles again. But it had been a mistake to ask her. The familiar sulky look dropped like a curtain over her face and she pulled away.

'Just give my message to Binny. That's all. Either you should understand what I want to tell you, or don't bother asking me questions.'

Even while she did her best to sound tough, tears of happiness were streaming down her face. In her world where there was so little hope, Mandy's birth was perhaps a small glimmer of joy. But the victory she alluded to perplexed me. Could 'they'—the unknown enemy—have wanted to abort Mandy? After all, hadn't Harpreet said that Sharda's child had been saved because it was a boy?

To binnyatwal@gmail.com

Hi when you take a break from admiring your baby do tell me a little more about your father and mother-in-law. I know that they were highly respected etc but what did you think of them and why did your parents want to marry you into this family?

Take care, simi

To simransingh@hotmail.com

Hi—This is Santosh once again. Binny is sleeping right now. When she wakes up I'll ask her to send you an email, but I think, really, we should let the past rest. My daughter has suffered enough. Had I known this would happen, do you think I would have taken the risk? I thought they would treat her like a princess. And oh yes, the baby kept her up all night!!!

NINE

20/9/07

It took a long time for me to get used to her absence. In some ways, of course, I never did. But because the Boys were now the centre of a new problem, our attention was a little diverted. It began with the drugs and got more and more serious till one day my mother decided that she would write to her old friend in Southall and find out if she could suggest a suitable 'good' girl who would wake my older brother out of his drug daze. Even though he was not her real son, my mother always worried about him. She thought that if he left the country, perhaps went away from his so-called friends, he would recover. She had also thought that Rahul could go away with him and his bride. Slowly perhaps the whole family could leave the Bhoot Bangla, away from the reign of my grandmother Beeji, and Santji.

So photographs began to be sent up and down by email. Since my parents could not operate the internet, I was called in to download the photographs. As they discussed the pros and cons of the girls, it was understood that there was no need for the shortlisted girls to meet Jitu. I think they were also a *little nervous, in case anyone found out about Sharda; it could damage the family reputation.*

Everyone liked Binny the best. Except the prospective bridegroom Jitu, who was too busy with his drugs to really care and, besides, he was often away at the farm. The idea was that Binny's passport would take Jitu abroad to a whole new life. He would forget what had happened with Sharda. (Funnily enough, everyone felt sorry for him about what he had to go through over Sharda: after all, he had loved her so much, and she had hurt everyone with her behaviour. Though, of course, he was part of the decision-making body at home and had gone along with whatever happened.)

Perhaps he genuinely felt bad about it because he would sometimes come into my room and cry, especially if he was drunk or stoned. He asked Sharda (who was still missing) to forgive him and kept saying that he was sorry. I would stroke his head and tell him everything would be all right but, of course, he knew and so did I that nothing would ever be the same.

So a date was fixed for his wedding. Jitu just had to show up for it. It was the same with his job. There was no need to work as my father had enough land for us to live well for the next five generations. Jitu would not become a taxi driver abroad but he could probably set up a small business. Or so my mother dreamt, as she knitted this elaborate plan for his marriage.

Binny landed just the day before the wedding. She was pretty, but not too pretty, just like her photographs. I was warned not to talk to her too much and to stay out of the way. Usually the boy's parents go as the baraat to the girl's side, but in our case the boy stayed put. My mother was so nervous about the black magic turning everything into ashes again that she even reduced her dowry demands drastically. Apart from a car for Jitu in the UK and a small apartment for the newly-marrieds to live separately, they asked for nothing. All the demands were met: Binny's parents were thrilled that their daughter was marrying into such a well-established family. After all, Binny's father had only been a floor manager at Nestle and my father was the equivalent of the owner of several chocolate factories in Jullundur. Binny's father was obviously lower down the pecking order. They had to listen to us.

It was the wedding of the decade, with celebrations that went on for weeks. I was also given a range of new clothes to wear. It now seems like a century ago, but it has been barely eleven months since the wedding. I kept thinking that the one person who would have enjoyed it the most had been wiped out of the family forever. Her favourite brother was getting married. Before the wedding, all photographs with Sharda had been removed so that no one would ask any awkward questions.

No one ever did, thanks to the non-stop partying and praying going on. Most people were too busy to wonder about missing daughters.

It was a call from my mother, late in the evening on my mobile, that brought me back to my parallel reality. The reality in which all I had to do was Find A Husband. Usually, I dismissed my mother's rants on the subject without listening.

But now I heard every word, and each one seemed to attack and diminish me as a person.

Why was a husband so necessary, what was it that he could give me that I could not myself find in this world? The thought of a pair of green eyes gazing at me quizzically was thrust into the background. He was a married man. I felt a twisting physical pain in the pit of my stomach. It made me even sharper with my mother.

'Mom, listen. Every man I have met so far has been self-obsessed and boring. Why do you want me to lead such a dull life?'

'Life is not all ha ha hee hee.' Ah, the classic desi hit below the belt. 'You have to take things seriously, but for you anything serious is boring. Think of me, I'll die without seeing the face of my grandchild.'

Often I wondered if my mother had any idea what my work entailed. She probably thought I was doing the bhangra all day with women prisoners. That too was my fault, of course. I had once taken her to a ghazal night in Tihar Jail and given her the lasting impression that prisoners have a really cushy time. They never even have to buy tickets for a musical performance, like the rest of us do.

I could not resist sniping back: 'Boring applies to the men I usually meet. Anyway, tell me, since you're so obsessed with dying, why didn't you finish me off at birth? Isn't female foeticide the final word on all arguments like this?'

'What a silly question. Of course I wanted to have a daughter. I would have been happy with anything, frankly. Your father was so busy working that it was a miracle you were born at all. But let me tell you, I got plenty of commiseration from the family. Your dadi even suggested that I don't feed you. So many women do that because if a child dies of malnutrition, you can't be charged with murder. You just say, she refused to feed, what can I do?'

I remembered the story of a woman in Tamil Nadu who confessed that she tried to kill her daughter by not nursing her. Then, tired of the sound of the baby crying, she took some poisonous juice from an oleander flower, mixed it with castor oil, and forced it down the child's throat. Eventually the crying stopped. The crying had bothered her more than the act of killing.

I could have told my mother of other equally simple methods. For instance, pushing paddy husk down a baby's throat would rupture the windpipe. Or there was suffocation. Other women who witnessed the birth or the killing were invariably on the side of the mother: they knew the taunts and trouble that would follow the birth of a daughter. And now, in the twenty-first century, female children were also being killed as part of a package deal, while within the womb, during the pre-natal check-up. This way no one would ever find out.

Tiring of her haranguing tone, I promised my mother that I would put an advertisement in the paper announcing my availability as a bride. She missed the sarcasm completely. She said she would send me a sample text of the advertisement since she had recently met someone who had actually found a husband on the worldwide web. My mother, who had till recently stoutly resisted being lured into using a mobile phone, was now willing to try any kind of technology, so long as she could see the 'face of her grandchild, like a chand ka tukda'. It was a fantasy, but no one could prevent her from dreaming, could they? Did she really think I was going to produce a grandchild for her at forty-five?

I went through Binny's letter again and was ashamed of my earlier suspicions, that she may have made Durga the scapegoat. It was obvious that the two girls had a genuine affection for each other. Perhaps my inability to understand this case had become such a hurdle that I was willing to doubt anyone's intentions. Durga's tears and her happy reaction to Mandakini's birth had been moving. After all, Durga had very few friends and no family. At least she could still get love and affection from one person.

I rang for some ice with my whisky as I settled down to look at my emails. The manager called to tell me that a journalist wanted to meet me and he was waiting outside. I looked at the clock, it was close to 9 p.m. Cheeky, especially as it was a male journalist, I thought. My earlier decision had been to stay away from the media, but now, after all the recent unsettling events, I thought I should get a local point of view on what was happening with the case. Besides, I felt quite reckless, especially after the whisky. And my resolution to forget a rather devastating pair of green eyes.

I asked him to come in and join me for a drink. I was tired of role playing. If these buggers wanted to be shocked by a woman imbibing alcohol, let them. I didn't even care if he put a four-column spread of me on the front page of the *Daily Awaaz*, whisky glass in hand.

The reporter, Gurmit Singh, a tall, serious looking boy with a blue turban and a dark straggly beard was escorted in, and to my surprise, settled quite happily for a glass of beer. He did not even seem shocked to see a middle-aged matron swilling alcohol all by herself. He had relocated from Mumbai, just about a year earlier, because his newspaper wanted to increase the local coverage and the circulation figures. We exchanged fond memories of walking down Marine Drive in the rain, watching cricket at the Wankhede Stadium and sipping tea at the Wellington Club. It established us as fellow travellers suitably at sea on the dusty streets of Jullundur, if I am permitted to mix my metaphors. As you can imagine, we were beginning to get along very well. It was, after all, my first relaxed evening, without looking over my shoulder for an unknown assassin or trying to read tea leaves for the names of murderers.

We talked for a while about the 'case'. To my surprise, he wanted to know if I was going to link it with Sharda. He appeared to know a lot about her, and confessed that he had independently been investigating all the characters involved, including Harpreet. It was a sobering thought, but I refused to let the haze of alcohol subside.

'Sharda disappeared five years ago, why would I make the link?'

He took out a letter from his pocket.

'I received this letter only about five months ago. Shall I read it to you, it's in Gurmukhi? Basically it asks, "Where is she?" It arrived before the murders.

'The sender is anonymous but he or she did send me this photograph, and there must have been a purpose behind it.'

He handed me the same picture I had seen, of Sharda on the bed. I gave it back to him. The letter in Gurmukhi reminded me of the handwriting in Sharda's notebooks. It had the same highly decorative flourishes. But I wasn't sure if I should mention the notebooks, which in any case were with Harpreet.

'Why didn't you publish your material?' I asked instead.

'My newspaper proprietor refused to print anything about it. This is a small town, Simranji, and everyone still has very great respect for Santji. I have a lot of information on him, and he was no saint. But no one wants to know. Besides, even Amarjitji says he doesn't know if this girl is Sharda, so what can I say? I just thought I should tell you about it.'

In true Jullundur style he added 'ji' after every name. I could see that Gurmit-from-Mumbai already knew how to win friends and influence people.

Someone had taken this photograph, made multiple copies and sent them out. As recently as five months ago. Did that mean Sharda was still alive? One photograph had even been left in Durga's room. It appeared meaningless now, even if it were an attempt at blackmail, as all the family members were dead anyway, and the last one was in judicial custody.

Unless Sharda had been taken away by someone else and the family was completely blameless and had been carefully targeted by a murderer who had not left a single fingerprint behind. In which case, Harpreet's story had holes the size of craters. He had been talking about the strained relations between Durga and her family, the anger in the girl, the loveless existence she led.

Yet, this information could be a significant clue to understanding the murders. Did the photograph enrage someone so much that they wanted to kill the whole family? Or was it sent out as a warning that the same fate awaited the rest of the family? That is, if we assumed that Sharda was dead. She may not be.

'Did you try to find her again?'

'I did, and the trail definitely led up to the Company Bagh house. She was taken there from the asylum. She may even have been kept there for a while, but her body was not among those killed, and now with the police investigation it's impossible to go there.'

'I did go there a few days back, but the house seemed empty, except for one domestic helper—Manubhai.'

'I have a strong suspicion that Durga may know where she is. Why don't you ask her?'

That was exactly what Amarjit had said.

'I have already asked and she didn't say anything. More than me, you should be able to find her,' I told him. 'And if you do, please tell me.'

So we agreed to become accomplices in trying to unravel the mystery.

As the bonhomie between us grew, there was a small troubling moment when he asked me if I could arrange an interview for him with Durga. It made me suspicious of his real motives, his eagerness to share his information. And of his charming interest in me. The interview with Durga would have been the pay-off for our little chat, I supposed. I gently told him that it was far too soon to disturb an already traumatized girl. Besides, it would be a breach of confidence. And perhaps even illegal.

He then wanted to know if I could be interviewed. For a full page Sunday Supplement. Wow. That was so much better than the four-line matrimonial advertisement I had promised my mother on the Classifieds page.

I promised to think about it, but told him that if he wanted to work on this investigation with me, everything would be strictly off the record. Until I told him he could go ahead and publish.

Once business was out of the way, I have to say I enjoyed the evening. In all honesty, he also helped to drown out the memory of the morning. He was a little young for me (by at least fifteen years) but what the hell, he wasn't boring. If Demi Moore could do it... unfortunately, I had oiled my hair and even removed my bindi and silver earrings. I was also wearing a shapeless track suit, otherwise, given my restlessness and reckless mood, who knows how the evening might have ended?

To <u>simransingh@hotmail.com</u>

Hi I am taking some time out while the baby is asleep as I know this is very important for the case. We must do everything to save Durga. I know its risky putting everything down on an email—but I feel time is running out, and there are certain things u must know, and know very soon. I don't know if any of this will be helpful, but...

Every time I see Mandy I realize how close I came to losing her, so I don't think I can keep quiet about it any more. The moment I arrived in Jullundur, I realized what an obsession these people have for their sons. Initially, of course, it didn't bother me too much, because I was allowed to do most things. But their attitude pissed me off. The way they treated Durga was bad enough, but one day I went down to the farm. There were two girls there, who had been brought in from Bihar. They cried when they saw me, because I tried to talk to them. U know, no one had tried to speak to them before. One of them even had children—and she didn't look any older than thirteen!

But it was the whole lifestyle there. If people came over, all the women sat on one side, and the men on the other. They didn't like it if u tried to speak to any of the men. It was a huge strain for me, but I knew we were going back after a few months and I could start leading my own life again. So why quarrel. My father had just had a heart attack, I didn't want him to get worse.

However, I had no idea why Santji was so mad keen on a grandson—after all, Rahul was around. I didn't quite know the connection but I knew that he had been sort of adopted by my in-laws even though I knew that my father-in-law was not too happy with that situation, either. So right from the beginning the pressure was on me to produce, produce, produce... like a fucking factory.

It was tough because Jitu was ardent all right but he wasn't David Beckham, u know what I mean? Needed a lot of coaxing. He was a big-built guy, but I've seen better erections, let me tell u. Sometimes he just went to sleep without even a conversation. I knew something was wrong. I caught him one day with the younger Bihari girl. He begged forgiveness and then... well, I got pregnant. The Bihari girl was really upset, she would look at me with such anger every time she came to the house and these strange voodoo dolls began to appear in my room. Limbless and pregnant. It was meant to be me, of course, but I didn't tell anyone, not even when the dolls appeared to be slashed and bloodstained. I also knew these things upset my mother-in-law who was really superstitious. I don't know who was doing it all. I still think it was Manubhai who was the prime instigator. Perhaps he thought his daughters would find a place in that house, if Jitu or Sanjay decided to acknowledge their relationship with them. You know how in India men have two wives and no one gives a shit.

In fact, everyone else seemed ok with the situation, till one day, after three months, I was asked to go with Santji for a test. I went along thinking it was about time I got a doctor involved. I was thinking of having the baby in the UK but they said they wanted me to have the baby in India.

They actually owned a nursing home close by, and that's where we went. I started feeling a bit strange, because my father-in-law came inside with me when they were doing my check-up. He said he wanted to know if I was all right.

I went red with embarrassment but he was very venerable, with his white beard and soft-spoken ways, so I just let it be. But then he insisted that I have an ultrasound. Now I know it's illegal to know the sex of the child in India, so I thought he wanted to find out if the baby was healthy so I went along with it all. But to my surprise, he said we had to wait for the report and not go home.

The doctor called us in and said it was going to be a normal baby girl. I was so happy that I almost jumped for joy until I saw my father-in-law's face.

He seemed very unhappy all the way home. At home, too, it was the same story. My mother-in-law went into her prayer room. That's when Durga and I had our first and perhaps last proper conversation.

It was clear to me that not only my life, but the life of my unborn child was in danger. Durga and I started planning my return to Southall. It was done very gradually, in bits and pieces, and in total secrecy. Frankly, I was scared of the whole lot of them. As a first step, I simply said I was going to Delhi as I wasn't feeling too well, to stay with my relatives for just a few days. Durga begged me to take Rahul along, and his passport. Luckily, as the whole family was to visit us later in the year, his passport was ready. She stole it from my ma-in-law's cupboard and gave it to me.

The pressure was already building on me to abort the baby. My father-in-law spoke about the need for a small compact family. My mother-in-law tried to tell me how it would be nice for my parents as well if the firstborn were a son. Jitu too began to parrot whatever his parents said. They were all worried about the division of the property. The matter of the small dowry was also brought up. It was meant to make me feel guilty. I just hung in there, in whatever way I could.

I was determined to leave with my pregnancy intact. They

tried to trick me into going to the clinic a few times, but I managed to fake headaches and morning sickness. Luckily, no one suspected anything. One week after I left, I was safely in Southall, and they were all dead. What can I say? It's a terrible coincidence, but it's the truth. I can only tell u what I said that day on camera. It is better this way.

I better go. She's crying. Give my love to Durga.

Binny

To binnyatwal@gmail.com

Thanks for the email. It's good to know what actually happened. And now I understand why Durga seems so angry with her parents. And why you are so grateful to her. I'm going to try to do my best to get her out.

Love, Simi

TEN

When I heard about the baby I thought I would die of
happiness. At least one child had been saved... though it
was not enough, not enough. It brought back too many
memories, the whispers of the servants, the things I could never
understand. How I slowly found out the most savage part
of my family history, how my great-grandmother had been
told that she would have to leave the main house when she
gave birth to her sixth daughter in a row. A great tradition
of culling out girl children that we maintain till today for
ourselves and for others through the clinics we run, where tests
are conducted and babies are aborted. They are buried without
fanfare in the fields around the house. Occasionally, while
tilling the land, tiny skeletons are turned up in the earth, but
the loyal family retainers never let anyone know. The bones
are quietly ground into dust or thrown into the river Beas.
Grateful families are only too glad to help cover up.

Once when I came back from school, Sharda took me to the
back of the house. I noticed the dirt beneath her fingernails.
Have you been working in the fields, I asked. Yes, she said.

Occasionally, they allowed us to help with the sowing and ploughing in the fields where we grew strawberries for export. Sometimes they even let me drive the tractor, and I made zig-zag troughs around the field, till Santji came out and scolded them. He was even more angry when he saw my turban and white trousers. He slapped me for 'telling lies' and told me to change into something more suitable for a girl.

Carefully, Sharda took out a paper envelope from which she drew out a tiny white skeletal hand. She made me hold it. I want you to know what they do in this house, Durga, she said. This hand was buried deep in the vegetable plot. There was also a tiny skull and other limbs but they have all been crushed by the tractor. This is the only thing that I managed to dig out. I would have been there too, if Jitu had not found me. You too, because like me, you refused to die. Why were we so stubborn, Durga? Why did we not accept a decent burial when it was given to us, instead of this hell day after day after day? She held me close, while I held that tiny hand, and we both cried. Something in those little helpless splayed out little fingers seemed to beckon me. The white spidery fingers were like small pieces of chalk, but they seemed to speak to us.

At first horrified, with a child's natural fear of death and ghosts, I slowly examined the tiny hand from which the flesh had been eaten away. Did she have a name? I asked Sharda. No, she said, there were too many of them and most of them died unnamed. I'd like to pretend she had a name, and a chance to grow up. The poor thing. We can only pretend, Durga. Will they do this to your baby? I asked. Only if it's a girl, she said, holding me even closer.

Cradling that hand still in my hand, like a precious flower, I

*gazed out at the innocent-looking field behind our house which
was now being readied for the next crop. As the furrows were
ploughed up between the tractor wheels and the cruel rake at
the back, I imagined the claws tearing away the flesh from tiny
bodies which never had a chance to cry out or draw their first
breath. It's like a battlefield, isn't it, Didi? I asked Sharda.
When soldiers die in the army, there must be thousands of
skeletons left behind.*

*She stroked my hair. Yes, but when that happens, people give
them medals and honour their families. These little babies...
no one even remembers them. Why should they bother?*

They could have been our sisters.

Overall, the meeting with my new journalist friend had
cheered me up immensely. At last I felt that I had someone
on my side. Also, he seemed to admire the work I did, and
even hoped to collaborate with me on an article on jail
reforms. When I came out from my room the next morning,
the disapproving guesthouse manager mumbled, 'There are
flowers for you, saar.'

Gurmit had sent flowers with a note that said, last night
had been one of the most enjoyable evenings he had spent
in Jullundur. I thought I knew the feeling, but decided not
to waste the elaborate bouquet woven through with roses
and green ferns.

I called for a rickshaw to visit Amrinder and give
her mother the flowers. There was no point in the red
roses adorning a guesthouse room where only I could admire

them. Also, I didn't quite want to get sentimental over a thirty-year-old. I knew enough women, including me, who had made fools of themselves over impossible relationships and I didn't want to be on that list again.

I carefully thought through what I should say to Amrinder. She had shown little desire to meet me, but I believed I still needed to find out what the gossip was about me and the case. I knew I was probably taking too long to make a breakthrough but people should understand it took time to win the trust of a suspicious fourteen-year-old who seemed to have even fewer friends in Jullundur than I did.

As I got deeper and deeper into the mystery, I knew the solution was just a few steps away. Only, I did not know which direction to take. The list of suspects just grew longer and longer. If anger were the motive, then the murderer could have been Harpreet, Binny or even Manubhai or his daughter. Perhaps there were others too, who knows?

Despite everything, I still felt a little calmer than I had for days.

Perhaps Amrinder could forget our past quarrels and help me?

Since it was morning and the school term was still on, Amrinder was alone at home with her mother who was resting in an easychair near her. The chemotherapy had made Ma Sukhi lose all her soft white hair, and her bald head glowed in the morning sun. Even though it was warm, a light quilt had been put around her shoulders and legs. She had been a large and loud woman who had always dominated parent-teacher meetings in school. It was tragic to see her reduced to a small, shrivelled bundle. But her mind seemed as sharp as ever. And her trained teaching voice as loud.

'Oye, Simran di bachchi, come here and give us a hug.'

I gently pecked her cheek. A stale smell of Ponds Dreamflower talc mingled with urine floated up from her. The indignities of growing old and incontinent. Who could imagine the fierce battleaxe begging for attention?

'Still troubling your poor mother, hanh? I heard you want to play all this social worker-social worker and not get married-sharried, hanh? Look at Amrinder, she always did better than you in school, remember. Even now, look at her, two lovely kids, lovely husband, lovely house and you... your hair is turning white and you think you can still run around like you are sixteen?'

There was no chance for me to even interrupt. Besides, every word was true, wasn't it?

Amrinder looked helplessly at me.

'Don't worry, aunty. I'm putting an ad in the papers. Might find a munda that way.'

'Don't you have a boyfriend by now?'

'Mother, leave her alone. She's come to see you, not to get lectured. Look at the lovely flowers she's got for you.'

'Very nice, but I feel sorry for her mother. First she is a widow, then she has this daughter...'

'Surely the other way round?'

'Don't be rude.' At last the round moon face broke into a smile. Thank god for her feisty spirit. It had kept her alive.

'I've come for help... you know, the Atwal case?'

'Arrey, those poor people. Those awful girls. Tauba tauba tauba. To kill your own parents. She was in love with that man, you know. That tutor. He had an affair with the sister and then he tried the same thing with her. She was under his spell.'

I looked at aunty's face. We called all women older than us 'aunty' in Punjab. And all older men were called 'uncle'. Earlier we had more complex terms to describe relationships, but with the coming of the colonizers and the angrezi craze, much of the descriptive terminology, such as phoopi or taayi, had been junked for an all-encompassing 'aunty', as we replaced more and more of our colourful Punjabi with a much blander English. She, of course, was no relation of mine, and right now, I was relieved about that. Her illness may have made her fragile, but she could still say the most cruel things.

Except, what she said had an ominous ring of truth to it. I could feel some more pieces of the jigsaw clang into place. The charm of the tutor had engulfed me too, the gentle manner, the intelligent soft face, those sad green eyes. I was obviously not the first to fall for him. I could feel the red blush of shame spread over my body once again. What a fool I was. A good-looking man only had to look at me once and I became like putty in his hands.

'So why did she kill her family?'

Amrinder shook her head. 'I think you've been away far too long. They would have never allowed her to marry him, you know.'

'But tell me, if the sister had already had an affair with the tutor, why would he be allowed to come into the house to teach the younger girl? Were they so stupid that they would allow the same mistake twice?'

'She met him outside. She knew where he lived.'

'Oh, come on. I've been to his house. He's a married man. He even has a young daughter. And Durga is only four years older than her!'

Amrinder gave me a pitying look. It was a look I remembered from school. We were old adversaries, after all, once upon a time pitted against each other, vying for the gold medal for the best student. Trying to beat each other to answer the teacher even before she could finish the question. Spending days on the school projects which would get us the required recognition… and into the teacher's good books. Theatre, elocution, anything and everything that could make us stand out. It was a desperate time, and now from her eyes I saw we were back in the boxing ring, circling each other. This time she had more at stake than me: her husband's career. If there was anything I knew, she had to get it out of me. As I sipped my nimbupani, I felt the adrenalin rush. This time I would be better prepared. Not like when she tried to snap the gold medal from me at the last minute. Not this time. I sat up straight and looked back at her.

'I don't understand you, Simran. You've been asked by Amarjit to talk to Durga, not prowl around Jullundur investigating, looking for tutors! You're a social worker, not a bloody detective! No wonder you're taking so long getting her to open up with the case.' Ma Sukhi's beady eyes swooped down on me.

Amrinder looked at me thoughtfully. 'The police are there to investigate, not you. They only want to know the truth from this girl about what happened that night. And for that they simply want you to tell them when she is ready to record her statement, when she is more emotionally stable, that's all. It's quite straightforward.'

I looked at the mother and daughter. I could not even begin to explain to them how I felt. My sorrow over Durga, my desire to rescue her, and all the other children like her.

For a moment I was back in school in the Principal's office, flushed from running down the corridor. Amrinder stood triumphantly on one side and her mother sat plump and supercilious in the chair opposite Mother Superior. In her hand, the Principal held a notebook. How had I forgotten that moment which changed my life forever? My pulse was racing and I felt I was losing the battle already.

'Of course I have been meeting her, but I also thought I should meet the other people involved so that I can sort it all out, and understand what the girl has to say. To ask her the right sort of questions.'

The thin cancer-ridden face smirked back at me, each wrinkle mocking my inexperience and stupidity. 'Arrey, Simran, silly, silly Simran. You'll always interfere, won't you? Always poke your nose into everything; when you have a whole police force behind you, you'll try to do better. Too intelligent for your own good. It didn't help you in the past, did it, this social work-social work. Remember when...' She looked at Amrinder and they both burst out laughing.

Things were rapidly spinning out of control. I had come in search of allies and found an old rivalry. A sickening feeling of dread swept over me. Mother Superior waving the notebook and my inability to speak. My desire to protect my friends, then the evidence spread on the table... It was the perfect set-up.

I got up abruptly. But I tried to keep my voice free of stress, and my face was bereft of any expression other than sympathy.

'Aunty, it's great to see you in such good spirits. Lovely to remember the old times... but I have to leave because I have to meet Durga. Good you reminded me of my real duties!'

I forced myself to kiss both of them goodbye. In this vitiated atmosphere, they must not think that I had any fears. Keep it light, I told myself grimly as we laughed and smiled and promised to meet again. Surprising how even death—or a terrible disease like cancer—does little to mellow some people. They still carry their burden of destruction with them, I thought, seeking to annihilate others before death snaps them in its jaws.

I needed a drink again but it was still early morning and I knew that I really had to be careful. Too many reputations hinged upon this case: recently, even the chief minister of Punjab had wanted to see the latest progress report. Any more meetings like the one today would mean I had finished my chances of helping Durga forever.

On my way to the jail, Amarjit's car passed me, siren blaring and red light flashing, even though the road was half empty, except for me in the rickshaw, a bullock cart and a creaky overloaded bus that slowly swung from side to side like an elephant in heat.

The car skidded to a halt in front of us and one of his minions, following in a jeep bristling with black commando uniforms and guns, waved at me to stop. I told the startled rickshawallah to pull up on the side.

Amarjit rolled down the dark windowpane and looked amused to see me with my jhola, crouched beneath the rickshaw hood, desperately trying to avoid the glare of the afternoon sun. He opened the door of his sleek black limousine and asked me to get in. After our recent cold conversations, I was relieved to see a smile on his face.

'Surely you can afford an air-conditioned car?'

'I like to suffer,' I replied, retaining my reputation as the village jester.

'I seem to remember that your father left you a large inheritance? There were houses and cars... have you run through the entire fortune so quickly?' He was teasing me because he knew I was upset over the distance he had maintained from me since I arrived. I pretended not to understand.

'Which is a convenient excuse not to pay me for my work, is it?'

'That's not fair. You're the one who said you don't take any hafta, your exact words.'

I could not help a reluctant laugh. It was familiar, this semi-flirtatious banter between Amarjit and me, a leftover from our college days when he fell in love with me and I fixed him up with my best friend. He said he never forgave me for it, though he eventually married her. After two children and a trial separation, they were just about together again, but lived in different cities. I never knew whose side I was on—even though surprisingly, I got along very well with both of them. Except when Amarjit used me as an excuse to leave his wife whenever the going got tough. Or, at least, that's what he had always told me. Even if it wasn't true, it was flattering to hear—that someone could, without asking for anything, love you unconditionally for over twenty years.

As for his wife, she knew I would never hurt her, so she took our friendship in the manner in which it was meant: something that never would and never could reach its full potential.

'I just had a dreadful session with Ma Sukhi, Amrinder's mom. She is still as bitter as they get and Amrinder is a regular branch off the old neem tree.'

'Her husband is due for a promotion. A lot rests on this case. So now you know.'

'I know. Amarjit... is there anything about this whole case that you feel I should have been told?'

For a moment, a rather weary expression crossed his face. He repeated what Amrinder had said to me thirty minutes ago.

'Had you been in this town and not left it twenty years ago, you would not have to ask that question.'

'Shall we have dinner and add to the local gossip?'

'I wish I could, but these latest bomb blasts mean we have a high-level security meeting with the prime minister tomorrow. In fact, I am driving down to Delhi right now, thought I would grab a quick chat with you when I saw you in that stupid rickshaw. I still miss you, you know.'

'Oh, well...' Inadvertently, I sat back and sighed, looking at him in despair. Amarjit is what is called a 'cut surd'. It means he remains a Sikh while being able to shave his beard. His is a rugged face, with a slightly crooked nose and thin, imprecisely set lips. His eyes darkened slightly as he gazed back at me. We had shared too many moments in the past not to be able to connect.

We had reached the remand home by now and while the guards saluted to let him in, we exchanged another long look and he raised his eyebrows. We could not say anything because we both knew the driver in the front seat would be listening avidly, and I wasn't quite sure what I was doing at that point. All I needed was some reassurance that I still had someone who would root for me, someone who believed in me. But then, having discovered that Amarjit was also involved in the cover-up after Sharda's disappearance, shouldn't I be more careful?

'One consolation you do have right now is that the bomb

blasts—and there has been one more in Jaipur today—have taken the attention away from the case. So you will have more time to sort it out. How is the girl? Has she told you anything?'

Mindful of the driver listening, he quickly added, 'You don't have to tell us anything she says, just let me know when we can record her statement.'

'She's told me very little. But we are being unfair to her, you know. She is still in depression.'

I was talking to the old Amarjit. The one I knew in college and university, who ate my masala dosa before I could even open my mouth.

'I know, don't worry. I'll get Amrinder and Ramnath off your back. At least for another ten days. But you know, these are very ambitious people, and this is a high-profile case. Just remember, I am the only one who wants to keep Durga out of jail. It would be very simple if... anyway, let's meet and talk when I get back.'

I ignored that last promise. He had assured me of ten more days, that was the most important thing.

I got out of the car with a sense of accomplishment. It was a relief to know that I had some breathing space to get closer to Durga and that I would not be pushed around, even though the ground reality remained unchanged. I squared my shoulders and walked in to meet her.

I had brought her a box of chocolates to celebrate Mandy's birth. I was trying to keep things as normal as possible, despite the bizarre situation. Fortunately, as the guards had seen me arrive in Amarjit's car, they let me in with the chocolates. They had got used to me by now and rarely frisked me.

Durga was already in the room, and like any child, her

eyes lit up at the sight of the box in my hands. Why hadn't I thought of it before? I must buy her more things, stop treating her like a convict who had to be deprived of everything. It's peculiar how jails wreck your normal patterns of purchase and consumption. Once inside, you assume that all choice must be immediately suspended in favour of dirty toilets, dark cells and watery maggot-ridden food. Of course, Durga was safe from complete degradation as yet, but I was suddenly very conscious that I held the key to the amount of time she could be kept away from the fate that Ramnath was convinced she deserved. Her very existence was going to be decided by the way I played out this case. How I presented it to Amarjit.

'Any particular flavour that you like?'

Durga seemed hesitant to express any preference.

'I like the orange flavoured chocolates,' I told her.

She shyly offered me one. I carefully broke off a small piece and, in turn, offered it to the constable who sat outside the door, half dozing in the afternoon sun. She smiled and took it.

'Did you read the book Harpreet sent you?'

She nodded.

'What was it?'

'It's a book of poems by Amrita Pritam.'

'Do you enjoy reading her?'

'And Shiv Kumar Batalvi.'

'Aren't you a bit young for that kind of poetry?'

Maye ni maye
Main ik shikra yaar banaya
Churi kuttan ta o khanda nahin
Weh asa dil da maas khawaya.

I remembered the lines from the time I lived on Batalvi's poetry. In English, they would roughly translate as:

O Mother, I have made a bird of prey my lover
When I give him bits of bread he doesn't eat
So I feed him with the flesh of my heart.

Shiv Kumar Batalvi—handsome, alcoholic Punjabi poet who died young—wrote dark romantic poetry, not quite meant for impressionable fourteen-year-old minds.

She shrugged and said shyly, 'My sister made me read them when I was younger. I guess my tastes were always more adult... it happens when you have a sister who is five years older. You're always trying to catch up. I was definitely more mature than the other girls in my class.'

'Did you study with Harpreet along with your sister?' I had to be very careful not to frighten her off, but Ma Sukhi's biting words still spun in my mind.

'I did, but only when I was... around nine or ten. After Sharda left, my lessons stopped.'

'He seems to like you a lot.'

'He's a nice man.' Her voice gave nothing away. Either she was a great actress or she was truly indifferent. Only the little tic at the corner of her mouth became slightly more noticeable.

'Did you meet his wife?'

'Never.'

'I saw her... when I went to his house. She looks like she was burnt.'

'It's her second marriage. She even had a daughter, but they tried to burn her because of the dowry. Harpreetsir married her because no one would accept her. Even her parents didn't want her back.'

'How do you know all this? I thought he married her only recently?'

There was a slight hesitation.

'I read about it in the newspaper.'

'Which one?'

'I don't remember. *Daily Awaaz*, I think.'

I was losing her.

'Did he come every day to the house when your sister was at home?'

'Why are you so interested in Harpreetsir?' Like any schoolgirl, she ran the two words together.

'I think he's an interesting person, and I thought you may want to talk a little bit about someone who cared for your sister.'

'How do you know that?'

'You must trust me. Everyone knows that. Your family was angry, they took Sharda away. I know where she went, I told you I had gone to the asylum. I even have a picture of her...'

I took the photograph of the emaciated Sharda out of my bag, watching her face carefully.

She looked at it and drew in her breath sharply.

'Didi.'

Her tears fell rapidly like the other day, but she did not make any sound. This was a child who had learnt to hide her tears, to cry without letting anyone else know. What must she have endured? I could see that she had suffered terribly—that she had known her sister's fate all along. It made me angry to see a child so helpless, possibly caught in a trap. Who had laid it for her? Who was the mastermind?

More and more, I was being irrevocably drawn to the conclusion that she was innocent. She was a hurt and angry child, no doubt, but there was also a softness to her and a deep weariness in every move she made. It was as though her life was over, and she was only marking time. Someone had used her and possibly continued to use her.

'Did you ever see her like that?'

'Only once.'

'Where?'

'At the house... my father was with her.'

'And this picture?'

I took out the photograph of the naked girl on the bed. For a moment she looked shocked. And then almost relieved.

'Where did you find this?'

'Amongst your books. Is this also your sister?'

She nodded her head. She seemed to want to say something more and then kept quiet.

'And do you know where it was taken?'

'No.'

'Can you guess?'

'Let me think about it. Can I go now, I'm very tired.'

I had already stored a scan of the picture on my laptop, so I let her keep the photograph.

'You should put it somewhere safe. It was also sent to some journalists, so I think maybe someone was blackmailing your parents. Perhaps they wanted to ruin their reputation? Or did someone kidnap your sister?'

She slid the photograph into the top lid of the chocolate box, and shut it firmly. Then she got up and slowly walked out. In her fourteen years, Durga had seen and experienced far, far too much.

౭౦

To binnyatwal@gmail.com

Hi just to let you know I had a good meeting with Durga and am finally able to understand some of the mystery. Will keep you informed. Send me Mandy's pix and will give to Durga. It will cheer her up. Simi.

To simransingh@hotmail.com

Grt news. Am attaching a pix of Mandy and Rahul together. My two lovely children. Please show these to my angel. Love

ELEVEN

22/9/07

*In many ways Sharda was the reason I found and lost myself
as well. She was like a mother, because after the encounter
with the skeletal spirit hand which was mine as much as
it was my sister's, I kept dreaming of the children my real
mother had buried. Ammiji, with her beautiful white face,
serene and calm, did not betray for a moment the angry
fingers with which my sisters had been killed.*

*She appeared so sprititual, spending her time in kirtan and
prayer. Only once had I seen her surreptitiously place flowers
on the ground at the back of the house where we had found
the spirit hand. After that she had been sent away on a
pilgrimage to repent.*

*There was no point talking about what Guru Nanak had said,
or all the equality rubbish that the TV was constantly blaring
out. Sikhism is one of the few religions that actually does
confer an equal status upon men and women. But the women
in our home were terrorized into accepting their inferior
position, and even an educated woman like my mother who
could discuss the suffragette movement and women's votes in a*

posh English accent had been beaten into submission. We all remembered the time she did not appear at the dining table, her eyes turned silently towards the window as she lay in bed till the scars healed. It was the way things were in the Bhoot Bangla and how they would remain forever. It was a moot point that she could have escaped and taken us all with her. But perhaps there was too much at stake for her.

She needed the status of a married woman, had never worked, and was terrified of exposing the truth to the world. She lacked the courage to undertake such a difficult journey. She did not want the world to know who my father really was, behind the mask he wore every day. The ignominy would have destroyed them.

To be honest, I still loved her. But from Sharda I learnt to temper the love. I removed from it all strands of hypocrisy and when I pared it down to the core, there was very little feeling left. I named my unborn and unknown sisters. I celebrated their birthdays and, with Sharda, I took eternal vows over searing candle flames that we would allow our daughters to live and love.

My father's biggest ally in all this was, of course, Beeji, his own mother, who did not conceal her deep dislike for her daughter-in-law's inability to produce a male heir. Maybe she was inordinately proud of her own robust and rapid production of three sons. Of the few children in between who were swept away on the waves of the Beas before they were able to talk or walk, very little was ever said.

One of them was rescued from the swirling waters and later returned to find out who her parents had been. Like Sharda and me, she had not been meant to survive. My grandmother refused to meet her and my father escorted her out. We never saw her again. She was among the unmentionables, of course, because Santji dictated everything in the house. It puzzled me that when we could all be turned into independent money-making machines—if they trained us to be engineers or doctors or stockbrokers—why did they want to destroy us over money or dowry or give us away in loveless marriages? It was not a question anyone could ask Santji because he had laid down the law. It had to do with family tradition, according to which a woman did not work outside the house. With each law that he laid down, he tormented my mother more and bought her silence.

Three daughters... Ultimately the number was revealed when I stumbled upon an ultrasound report hidden in my father's desk. My great-grandmother's curse. The fear of a second wife had snatched away all her arguments. But my mother was even more unlucky: two of her daughters survived so that she could be humiliated daily by her mother-in-law who kept up a litany of lament and abuse. Two of the lost children had been early abortions, but where was the third? I took out the tiny hand from the pencil box in which I had kept it and stroked it. Somehow its determination not to disintegrate into the earth seemed linked to my own survival.

What had been my story? I imagined myself—a tiny child, as yet not even able to suckle—being fed opium. I probably went to sleep, and they may have thought I was dead. It was only when they began to bury me in the ground that my sudden shriek made Amla run because she thought I was a ghost. I can still feel the earth being shovelled onto me. Sometimes in

*my nightmares the mud descends on my face, handfuls of dirt
are shoved into my mouth and in my eyes. Breathless, I gulp
for air and fight the bed sheets. When Sharda was around,
she would stroke my face and calm me down. She brushed
the imaginary earth from my face and blew breath into my
struggling mouth with her own. Drawing deeply on her oxygen,
my mouth stuck to hers, my lips pressed to hers, my body
clinging to hers and my tongue on her tongue, I learnt to live
because she knew and I knew that we could only take what
small portions had been kept aside for us and we never knew
when it would all be snatched away.*

I returned to the house in Company Bagh with a clear mission
to find out what could have happened to Sharda. Somehow I
thought the answer lay in the room I had found her books in.
Or perhaps within the mysterious annexe at the back, which
I hadn't even got to. Or the well in front of the house. Was
it still being used?

There is an eerie quality to a disused well. Years ago, the
well in our old house in Jullundur had been used to water the
small vegetable patch and I had been fascinated by the way
the Ferris wheel moved up and down as the bullock yoked
to it trod steadily round it in circles. The water, despite the
leaves covering it and the moss that grew on the side, had a
particularly sweet taste, which no tap water ever had.

Nostalgically, I stopped by the silent well at Company
Bagh to peer into its depths. Nothing. The well was bone dry.
I knew the ground water levels had fallen in Punjab thanks
to an inadequate monsoon, but this was a surprise. Not even

a small pool of water. There was only a damp darkness and a slightly foul smell, as though some animal had fallen into it. The guards watched me indulgently from the door.

I knew what they were thinking. This woman is going to jump in and make our day. I was going to disappoint them.

I strolled up to them and noticed that there were a few more cars, including a police jeep, parked at the entrance. Unlike the other day, they probably thought I was part of the group already indoors and let me in without too many questions, once I mentioned the magic names of Amarjit and Ramnath.

Walking in, I felt a change in the environment. It was no longer as musty as it had been the other day. I saw immediately that the dustcovers had all been removed. Someone had been working on the stains on the wall, they appeared to have been painted over. Hadn't Amarjit told me the evidence would not be tampered with? A little further down, the door to Sharda's room was open and I could hear voices.

I went closer and found another surprise. It was Gurmit Singh of the floral bouquet talking to someone who had his back towards me. Another beautiful friendship bites the dust. It hadn't taken him long to get his exclusive Sunday Supplement interview, and it certainly wasn't with me. They were both so involved in their conversation that they did not see me. Ramnath was posing at the door, pointing at the bed.

'This was the room where she was found, tied to the bed. She said she had been raped, but it was a very loose knot. The question is, why didn't she escape?'

He spoke while the photographer clicked away. I quickly

moved out of the way. But I heard Gurmit's next question as he furiously wrote in his notebook.

'And you are sure of her guilt?'

'Absolutely. We have so much evidence that the court will have no problem. It was difficult to solve, but somehow we have managed it.'

His words were completely against the tenets of justice which proclaimed that everyone was innocent until proven guilty. But the hunger for headlines and quick publicity had thrown ethics to the winds. His self-congratulatory tone made me feel like breaking up the party, but I had come here for a different purpose. I wanted this inert structure of a house to reveal its secrets. Somewhere, hidden in this space, was the real story of what happened that night. I knew I had no jurisdiction to object over the removal of evidence, and if I said anything in front of Gurmit, or if I even appeared in the story, it could become contentious. This was Ramnath's big moment and I couldn't wreck it.

For a split second, though, I did want to ruin his day. I was especially tempted when I thought of Amrinder and Ma Sukhi. I imagined their faces and their disappointment over Ramnath's lost chance. But I resolutely turned around and forced myself to walk down the corridor, away from the interview. At the other end, I found myself in a long, multi-pillared veranda that overlooked a large field that had been prepared for sowing. Now it lay fallow as obviously the owners had left no instructions regarding what to plant. There was no sign of Manubhai but I was curious about the dogs, who were quiet today, and of course, Manubhai's daughters.

The servants' quarters, like in most large homes, lay at the back somewhere. I opened and closed the doors as I passed, trying to register the geography of the house inside my head. There was one room in which a Guru Granth Sahib still lay open on a page. They say that if you open it early in the morning with a prayerful heart, you will get what is called a 'hukumnama', or the instructions for the day. I wondered what the family had read the day they had all been killed.

The poison had been fed to them, mixed in their food, strong doses of it. In fact, much more than what Durga had bought. I walked into the kitchen and imagined that evening. The servants were conveniently on leave, the food had already been cooked. So during the reheating, or perhaps earlier in the day, was when the poison had been slipped in. Or, at least, that was the police hypothesis. The obvious question then was, did Durga have an accomplice? Or did she do it at all? As I looked around the vast kitchen and the dining table, I felt more and more strongly that Durga could not have managed it alone. Yet the police were not even looking for a second or even third suspect.

When the family sat down to dinner, how did she escape? From what I remembered, she had said she wasn't well, and had gone to her room to sleep before dinner. I traced my footsteps to the dining room, and then mentally imagined Durga already in her own room. What was she doing? Couldn't she hear the sounds of people crying out, perhaps for help? She said she had been drugged, poisoned and then raped. The police files were silent on the drugs, but she had shown traces of poison and signs of either violent intercourse or rape. Of course, it had been raining all evening so the noise of thunder and rain could have covered up both her cries and those of the family dying in the house.

In the dining room there would have been chaos, with

vomit and blood all over the floor, which was how one of the dogs must have died, after licking the floor. But then, why the fire? Who started the fire? Why the stabbing? Were they not already dead? There is a theory that if someone stabs a person in this senseless multiple fashion, it could be due to mental illness or a deep desire for revenge. Could a frail fourteen-year-old, even if she was very disturbed, manage this sort of cruelty? Or was she being framed?

That could be why the stains had been removed from the wall, because someone wanted to remove the evidence of the actual mayhem. Especially if, apart from Durga, there were others involved. Who were the others? As I walked around the drawing room, I tried to imagine that evening.

Where was Manubhai? And where were his daughters? I thought back to what an overwrought Durga had told me about Manubhai. One of the girls had been kept in a room close to Jitu's. *To keep him there. To tie him down. Even after he was married.* I thought I heard someone whisper the words. But of course, it was only my imagination.

At the back, in the servants' quarters, the same desolate silence ruled. These were smaller rooms set beyond the house adjoining the barren field. The windows and doors of the rooms were closed but everything was clean as though the inhabitants had been here just a while ago. I opened one of the doors which had been loosely latched and found a darkened room, with a child's doll on the ground. The doll was made of cloth and had a needle stuck in it. I turned it around. There was a brown stain on the other side. The doll's face had no features.

'Oh, hello. This is a surprise,' said an unsurprised voice behind me as Ramnath tapped me on my shoulder. I jumped and turned, shocked and nervous at the unexpected interruption.

He looked at the doll in my hand.

'Where did you get that?'

'On the floor.'

'Can I have it?' He turned it around, and started laughing. 'God, these people and their black magic. They never give up.'

Behind him Gurmit entered the room and had the good grace to look a little sheepish.

'Not for the story, old chap,' Ramnath said. 'But this is what that poor Mrs Atwal used to worry about all the time, that someone was doing voodoo on her. All rubbish, of course, but we did find this sort of stuff lying around the house. However, this is only for your information... I don't want a murderer from the other world—ghosts are difficult to catch!' He chuckled and handed the doll over to one of the constables with him.

'Hope you didn't put it there?' he asked me jovially.

I refused to be provoked and answered, 'I was looking for Manubhai. I wanted someone to show me around the house properly. So far, I've just wandered around on my own.'

'I think he's gone back to Bihar.'

I found that strange as I had earlier noticed luggage lying inside the rooms. Vegetables, as though meant to be cooked, were still near the stove, and a few clothes were drying on the washing line. Manubhai, or whoever lived here, must have left in a great hurry. I shrugged resignedly.

'I see. Well, I'll just look around and then leave.'

I backed away from Ramnath and trudged back to the house, after an airy wave at Gurmit.

'Good to see you again.'

'You know each other?' Ramnath was immediately suspicious.

'Oh, just bumped into each other a few days back. I am just getting to know him,' I said quickly and deliberately and turned to leave. Gurmit opened his mouth to say something, and then after glancing at Ramnath, shut it again. Wisely.

On my bumpy rickshaw ride back, I remembered what Binny had said. The two girls from Bihar used to be kept at the farm most of the time. Now where could I find the Atwal farm? I hoped it wasn't too far, but first I would have to get the address from the police files. There was no point asking Ramnath, as no doubt he would try to stop me.

Back at the guesthouse, I found that the broadband wasn't working, so I couldn't access the internet. I knew Binny must have sent me the photographs of the children for Durga, but they would have to wait. I quickly glanced through my notes for the address of the farm.

The location, I realized, was en route to Amritsar, two hours from here. A visit would take me the whole day and I would probably not be able to meet Durga if I left immediately. So, even though it was Sunday the next day, I decided to see her and then leave for the farm.

Another night of drinking helped me to forget some of my anger at Gurmit. I kept my phone off the hook since I did not want to speak to him, and something told me he would try to call.

The next morning, getting ready to meet Durga, I chose a few books from the ones I had with me, which I thought she might enjoy. These included a random selection of short stories and essays which would not disturb her. I had the latest translation of Amrita Pritam's autobiography and took that along as well.

At the remand home, I discovered that Ramnath was five steps ahead of me. What I had dreaded had actually happened. Only a fool like me could have imagined everyone would stick to their word.

New instructions had been issued, I was told, by Ramnath Singh who was in charge in Amarjit's absence.

It had been decided that Durga had to be moved out temporarily.

The woman constable who gave me the information was extremely courteous and polite, but said she did not know where Durga had been moved. I remembered Amarjit's promise of giving me another ten days.

Was he part of this obfuscation? Why pretend to be friends at all? Why, indeed, this abrupt shift? It was frustrating and disturbing: Durga was opening up and was beginning to trust me, though very, very slowly. Taking her away at this crucial juncture was bloody unfair.

I felt an increasing sense of urgency, panic and anger. Why had I foolishly trusted Amarjit? I dialled his number from the jail, but it kept ringing. At the third try, someone picked up and said he was in a high-level security meeting in Delhi.

To simransingh@hotmail.com

Dear dear dear Simi, I haven't heard from u since yesterday. I do hope u are all right. No news of how u liked my two babies. Isn't Rahul cute? But of course Mandy is like Miss World. I wanted to tell you I got a strange call from Harpreet or Harpreetsir as Durga used to call him. I told u I had never met him, but now he called and said he is arranging a visa for the UK as he wants to visit us, and especially meet Rahul. I don't know what interest he cld possibly have in Rahul but it is getting me worried as I have already set up the adoption papers and I don't want any more complications. This child has suffered enough, and Durga will never forgive me if anything happens to him. I had not told anyone he was with me, even when the Press visited I kept him out of the picture completely. I am sorry to sound so hysterical but right now I am very nervous—I wish I had never contacted him about the letter I wanted to send to u etc, as I suspect he may have read it. I don't trust any one of them there, and I can't tell u often enough to be very careful.

Oh yes, he said that his visa could be fast-tracked because Ramnath who is also involved in Durga's case is a good friend of his. That is the only thing which gives me some hope, as I think if he is genuinely fond of Durga, then he may also get Ramnath to treat Durga properly.

Yet I wish, I wish I hadn't said anything about Rahul in my email or letters. U were the first to know that he is with me. Perhaps the cops knew but so far no one had said anything to me. Anyway, hopefully I am worrying over nothing. Diwali is round the corner and we'll all celebrate in Southall too, and I'll get Rahul some nice crackers. Do get Durga a pretty set of clothes (lime green is her favourite colour) and light a lamp with her.

Write soon, I depend on your emails. Luv from me, Mands and Rahul.

TWELVE

*It has been a strange day. After I got Sharda's photograph
from you, I kept looking at it and crying because it brought
back too many memories of my helplessness when that picture
was taken. Her lying on that bed, handcuffed to the side, not
even allowed any clothes or food, a long chain keeping her
from wandering too far away. You can't see any of that in the
photograph, nor can you smell the filth and dirt... She would
be like that for days, her faeces mixed with menstrual blood
lining the floor till someone came and cleaned it up. Why
did they do this to her? Her own family, her own flesh and
blood?*

*And why did Didi not die, though they must have tried over
and over again to starve her and beat her? It was not just her
indestructible spirit, it was also because of me.*

*She kept herself alive because she knew I was out there
somewhere, she had to make sure I grew up and made good.*

*She had promised me that, over the candle flame, when she
gave me the tiny spirit hand. I'll always be there, she said, they
will never kill me.*

Even after she forgot everything, even after the electric shocks and the beatings and the pills which made her sleep for days, she kept my memory somewhere deep within her, she could not give up.

Nor could I give up on her. Just that one brief time I saw her convinced me that I had to save her somehow... whatever was left of her.

But I who was so careful with Didi's memory slipped up today. The warden found her photograph in the box. After a while Ramnath Singh came, with his familiar simpering manner, his perfectly ironed clothes and slicked back hair.

He used to visit us in the house so often, looking at the chandeliers, eyeing the cutglass, putting a price on everything. It was he who encouraged Jitu and Sanjay when they wanted a 'hit'. I saw him, so many times, sitting in Jitu's room, talking softly, when my parents were asleep or away. He would sit, relaxed and impeccably dressed in a blazer and grey trousers, with a long drink of single malt whisky, while Jitu lay on the bed in a daze of opium and marijuana.

My mother thought he would be a good influence, and it was to him that my father turned when Sharda fell pregnant. In fact, it was he who had triumphantly brought the news.

I remember rushing out when I heard my mother cry out. It was the first time that my father had slapped her in front of a stranger, if you could call Ramnath that because now, of course, he was more of a confidante. He knew one of the family's worst secrets and he was going to decide Sharda's fate.

It took a while, and long conferences, and discussions of money because, of course, all the solutions required to be paid for.

People to be paid, doctors to be bribed and there was the most important question—where would Didi be kept while all this was going on? That was when they decided that they would leave it all to Ramnath. He would decide the twists in the story.

And when my mother objected—no, no, no, not that, not ever, ever that, not my daughter—my father slapped her in public. The message got through.

I was told nothing. Because Didi was locked up in another room, I had to hunt around for information. What were they going to do with her?

But I never knew, I never found out till they took her away. And because Jitu was with her, I never thought they would harm her in any way.

I could not have been more wrong.

So when Ramnath appeared today, I knew what was to happen. I was prepared. I don't think I was scared at all.

'There were six calls from Gurmitsinghji, saar,' said the gloomy manager who was clearly overwhelmed by my fast and loose life, when I finally returned to the guesthouse, dismayed at the sudden turn of events at the jail and worried about Durga.

I should keep my mobile phone switched on and not torture the poor man, I thought. All these strange quirks I had were part of the simple lifestyle I tried to adhere to—bolstered, of course, by my drinking, which was the only thing I did in excess.

My harebrained idea was to live as independently as possible and use technology only when it was required. Also, though I did not receive a salary or 'hafta' (as I had told Amarjit) for my work, since it was entirely voluntary, I still felt guilty spending the money my father had left me, which had been assiduously accumulated in his lifetime. I allowed myself to use just the bare minimum that would get me through.

He had been a man pushed to the limits of his ambition. Twenty-five years of setting up automobile spare part factories in small towns had made sure that his arteries clogged on the steady diet of petrol fumes and dusty by-lanes. He had dreamt of taking us to the Louvre in Paris and to the Black Forest in Vienna, but he never got the chance. In his wallet he would carry photographs of the house his father had owned in Lahore, a palatial double-storeyed home which was burnt down during the riots following Partition. His father's head had been neatly sliced from his torso and had landed at the feet of my startled grandmother, while they were escaping from the backdoor of the house with twenty-four balconies in 1947.

Ultimately, in a family of eight, only my father survived because he had the good sense to faint at the sight of all the blood and was assumed dead by the rioting mobs.

My father had never forgotten the lifestyle he had once known and neither had my mother let him forget it. She knew she could have been married to a millionaire's son but instead she had married, like thousands of other women with little choice at the time, a penniless refugee. So my father worked astonishingly long hours to build an empire with true Punjabi grit.

As I grew up, and he died, I felt a deep sense of shame

using his money without paying him back in some way. He had kept only three pairs of trousers and six shirts in his wardrobe. My mother had five cupboards full of clothes she had carefully collected, something for every fashion and every season. My father had never had time to watch television, go on holidays or play golf. My mother spent her time at ladies' lunches and the races, as well as the Gymkhana Club and the beauty parlour. She bought jewellery like people buy vegetables. It was a necessity, not a luxury. As I saw her teeter around in expensive high heels, I knew I could never get into her shoes. And how she resented that.

I was supposed to be the prettiest, brightest, most eligible girl in the city, but I had decided to become a khadi-clad, uninteresting NGO-wali. The lowest point had been when I rejected the millions of The Last Boyfriend.

I tried my computer again. The broadband was still not working, though the manager said he had complained about it. I charged my mobile phone finally and poured myself a beer. Tomorrow would be a difficult day, because I didn't know where they had taken Durga. I wondered if I should risk calling Ramnath. But if he slammed the phone down, or if there was a confrontation, I would be officially off the case forever.

As soon as I switched my phone on, it rang. Mother.

She sounded excited. 'I put the advertisement in the papers and already there are three proposals.'

'Only three?' I sat back and took a long gulp of the cold beer. It was still quite early in the morning, but I needed to calm myself. I also knew this would be a long conversation. How could I cut it short without her blood pressure shooting up?

'Darling,' she said (she hadn't called me that for six years!), 'that's great! One sounds really good. He's a divorcee with three children, but settled in the US. Just wants a simple Indian Jat Sikh girl. He says she should be fair but I think when he sees you, he'll know that's not important.'

'Of course, he sounds like he's made in heaven and we will make a perfect pair. But he should specify the colour of his complexion as well.'

'Now don't get uppity. What do you expect? Brad Pitt?'

'Mother, why don't you wait for a few more responses? I'll be home soon, and then we can spend all our time replying to all those lovely men, hmmm?'

Humouring her might work.

'I read about your case, you know, it's all over the Sunday papers. It seems the girl has done it. Something about the older sister having been in the lunatic asylum. I think they said she must be mental...' Mental in Punglish means a lunatic. My beer started tasting like horse piss.

I sat up straight and put the glass down. The one day I didn't read the papers, I got news like this. I knew now where they had taken Durga. Even as Mother rambled on with the details, I cut in as gently as I could and said I would speak to her later. Then I dialled Gurmit's number.

His voice was sombre as he picked up the phone. 'I'm sorry about yesterday, I wanted to tell you that there was a lot of pressure from editorial. They were adamant about running a special feature.'

'Congratulations. I believe it's a sellout?'

'Look, I know you wanted to wait, but the police are very certain that...'

I cut in. 'Thanks for your intervention. She's been taken away and I don't even know where she is.'

He seemed shocked. 'What? But Ramnath said he was going to treat her with kid gloves because she was so traumatized.'

'Why did you put in that bit about Sharda? Did you use the photograph?'

'No, but Ramnath provided all the details about her being locked up in Amritsar. I mean, I knew something was wrong when I received that picture...'

'You still don't know who sent it to you?'

'No.'

'Bad journalism.'

'No... I do have my suspicions. But I need to live in this town. If it's any consolation, I don't think this story is over. There was something very strange in the way Ramnath wanted to get all the kudos. He had orchestrated the whole thing so that there was no one else with us. He was the star. If you put the TV on, you will see him there again. He's on every channel. The case is solved, according to him. And he solved it.'

'Why has he shifted Durga? I thought there was a court order?'

'The order was to keep her in a safe place, with psychiatric help, but not locked up in a cell with other criminals. But if they concoct a story about her, they can take her anywhere.'

'I'm going to look for her tomorrow. But I want you to keep your mobile phone on, just in case I find something. One request, sincerely meant: please don't betray me the second time round. You know I am very worried about Durga. You also know that Sharda disappeared and has not been seen for the last five years. It is so easy to do that out here. And there is no one who really cares.'

'Have you asked the tutor?'

'Harpreetsir?' I found myself speaking like Durga.

'He called Ramnath while we were doing the interview. He wants help with his visa to go to the UK.'

'What? I mean why, did he say why?' Somehow I thought he was no longer involved in the case.

Gurmit did not know. I thought of those intense green eyes. That handsome, gentle face. The nervousness I felt when I looked at him, the perfect specimen of an intelligent, idealistic human being... someone who even married to uphold his ideals. Was there anyone in this small town who was straight or transparent about their motives?

'Can you do me a favour, Gurmit? If you are still in office, can you do an internet search and find out if there has ever been any newspaper article about Harpreetsir? I want to know. Call me back.'

He called back in ten minutes. Nothing on Harpreetsir. Durga had lied to me, she had said that she learnt all the details about his marriage from the newspapers. What a lovely story to touch the heart of a young girl; my own forty-five-year-old heart splintered with a bitterness I didn't know I could still feel. Why had he wanted her sympathy, and how well did she know him?

Even the whisky was not enough to drown the poisonous envy I felt. But I still had to find her. I owed her that much. And Harpreetsir? I wasn't sure I could trust myself to talk to him tonight. Too much was happening and much too fast.

∽

To <u>simransingh@hotmail.com</u>

dear simi - where are u? i am really worried. i saw a tv story and an interview with ramnath that they think durga may be crazy and that's why she killed everyone. that's rubbish. please stop this. why have u disappeared. please set the record straight. i know her, i know she is all right.

if they decide that she is crazy—i don't know how we can ever save her. how many years would she be locked up for and will she get any proper help? i wish i could come down there. to be on the safe side i am trying to fast track rahul's adoption papers. i don't know why harpreetsir is showing so much interest in him, and its making me very very nervous. the tv channels are calling me again but i have told them that i'm not well. please write to me or send me your number so I can call u.

u know my daughter and i are alive because of durga—she saved us. please understand that they would have forced me into that abortion, to get rid of my lovely mandy even though it is illegal.

please write soon. i am really worried about my angel, the poor thing, she must be so alone. luv binny.

THIRTEEN

I don't know the date or the day. I haven't felt so sleepy and tired in a long time. I think they gave me an injection, and I don't remember very much after that. When I woke up, I was in this room which is smaller than the one I was in before. In the previous one, there was a TV and a desk to write on. A cupboard. But here there is only my bed and a chair. I am lying on the bed right now, they have opened the bandages on my hands.

At night they had tied my hands to the bed, I don't know why. In the morning a doctor came and took my temperature and my pulse, as though I was sick. But I am fine. Even my clothes are still lying packed in my suitcase. I am writing this as fast as I can so my handwriting is a scrawl because I know they will give me another injection soon. I don't know where I am and how long I am going to be here. I will have to hide these papers carefully in between the clothes. I can't find any of the other papers I had written for you. I wonder if you will be able to find me. Did they tell you where they are taking me? Why didn't you come for me? I thought I could trust you. Did I say or do something to upset you?

Why did you give me Sharda's picture? Why was Ramnath so angry to see it? After all, he took the photograph. I have never seen him so angry. He hit me, and then someone put a black cloth over my head. I tried to fight them but couldn't. I finally blacked out because there was so much pain. I want to cry, but I am beginning to feel sleepy again. I can't do anything but sleep.

I had a restless night wondering what the day would be like. I had booked a car, taking care not to reveal my real destination as I realized that perhaps I had been a little too trusting. I told the guesthouse manager I wanted to go to Patiala. Clever, what? Throw people completely off the scent. Amarjit was still unavailable and I had asked for the morning papers so that I could go through the details of any fresh revelations. Luckily there was nothing new this morning, except for another terrorist attack, this time in Bangalore or Bengaluru as it was now called. Which meant that I probably would not be able to speak to Amarjit for a few more days.

I took a careful look around my room for anything incriminating. I wanted to carry all my notes, my files, everything, with me. I was quite sure that the broadband connection had been cut deliberately as this was the third day that it was not working. There was no time this morning to go hunting for an internet café. I would ask Gurmit to check my email. I called him and gave him my password. He promised to look at it as soon as he reached his office.

No doubt, after I left, my room would be searched. My suspicions had been aroused when I found some files lying on top of my suitcase and not inside where I had left them, when I returned from the jail yesterday. I imagined Ramnath coming in and smirking as he saw the pile of empty bottles lying on one side. He would be curious about what information I had gathered. Maybe disappointed to find so little. I imagined him laughing about it with Amrinder and Ma Sukhi. How wonderful that they could get rid of me yet again. Just like the previous time.

Oh, she would certainly have told him, along with Ma Sukhi. Silly, silly Simran was always an oddball. Very careless. You don't need to worry about her *at all*. You know she almost got the gold medal for the best student in school but she is such a silly billy. When the final school project was submitted for external assessment, both she and another girl had the same essay, word for word! Ditto. And you know, Ma Sukhi happened to be the external examiner. Which was how we found out. And then the two notebooks were presented and it was never clear which girl had copied, and you know poor Simran lost the gold medal to you know who. I was there in the Mother Superior's office, I wouldn't have missed it for anything. I saw her stuttering and stammering, but she couldn't say anything.

Silly, silly Simran could not say anything because the girl who copied her essay happened to be her best friend. It was a foolish thing, a schoolgirl prank which would have been ignored, except that the stakes were very high, so it couldn't go unnoticed. Neither did silly, silly Simran have the guts to confront her friend about it, nor did she tell the school that her notebook had been accidentally 'borrowed' by her friend for a few days. It went against her grain to do so.

So how did a gold medal matter? Well, it would have

been the culmination of a year of bloody hard work in school. And it would have meant a lot to her if her father had seen her get the medal. He died a few months later.

Somehow, silly Simran kept trying to make it up to her very absent and very dead father after that. Did everything she thought he would have liked her to do, the social work, the frugal lifestyle. Like I said, one stupid mistake changed an entire life.

From a promising bright student, I became a cheat and slunk around school corridors. Amrinder made sure everyone got to know, and the doubts remained. No one really believed I could have done it, as they knew I was bright and the essay was written in my style, but in small-town schools gossip is limited, so I provided the fodder for it for a long, long time.

How did it matter twenty-five years later?

The unshakeable memory of public humiliation, that was all.

Strange how life was once again pitting me against Amrinder. I just hoped I was clever enough to withstand the assault that I knew would be aimed at me.

I got into the car and told the surprised driver that we were going to Amritsar. In my new cautious avatar I would inform him of our actual destination only when required. It was a lovely morning. It had rained during the night and the air was still laden with fresh moisture and the scent of damp earth. But the sunshine paled as I thought of poor Durga. My instinct said that I was on the right track.

Perhaps I should first visit the asylum to prevent them from inflicting any further harm on her. But I knew I should first check the farm. Just in case.

My phone rang. For once I had kept it charged because I didn't know what the day would bring. It was Amarjit.

'Where are you?'

'Oh, out on a drive. I thought I would visit Patiala and meet some old friends, as your minions have deprived me of the job you had given me.'

'What do you mean?'

'That's why I called you. Durga has been shifted, and I don't know where she is.'

'Listen, calm down. I can tell from your voice you're upset. I'll explain everything when I get back. I got a message from Ramnath that she was becoming violent and they didn't know how to control her, so could they put her in a safer place.'

'Violent? I met her just before she vanished, she's one of the most docile children I have ever met. I know that she has been manipulated throughout this episode by someone. And I saw her earlier on Saturday, she was absolutely fine. I gave her Sharda's picture and she cried. For god's sake, this is a traumatized child. Will you guys get off her case and leave her alone? Where have you taken her?'

'Simran, right now I need to focus on my work here in Delhi. But I wanted to say that in case you need any kind of help, let me know. I'm worried about you. Stay out of Ramnath's way. He's a very ambitious man.'

'So?'

'Well, I was told that perhaps your internet connection had been cut off.'

'Did they tell you before they did it? You forget I'm in your guesthouse. Punjab police, remember? I should be safe.'

'I had asked you to come for this project, but others there are not so happy. Let me know if there is anything I can do. Just be careful and don't take any risks, okay?'

Suddenly, I was no longer worried about what was going to happen. I knew I could sail into the sunset on my own.

'Will you remember just one thing?' I was speaking very calmly for someone who felt as though she was in the middle of a full-scale war.

'I almost loved you in college. You were the coolest guy I knew, and I always wondered if by giving you up I had—' I stopped as my eyes filled with tears. 'But guess what? You had no balls then and you still don't.'

'I don't understand.'

'If you really wanted to protect me, you would not make such a big production of it. You know what's happening, Amarjit, and maybe you're even orchestrating it. But let me tell you that even though I left this town twenty years ago, I still know it inside out.'

I rang off and stared out at the mustard fields. Yellow. The colour of the man I had been talking to. I wiped away my tears of disappointment and immediately felt relieved at my own insouciance. Saying goodbye to Amarjit freed me, and I no longer felt responsible towards him. From now on I had to find my own solutions, in my own fashion.

I was prepared for whatever was going to happen, I only hoped I would come home with Durga at the end of the day.

The road to the Atwal farmhouse was bumpy, to say the least. I was jolted within every bone of my body, as the muddy pebble-strewn path masquerading as a road turned and twisted. The wall around the farmhouse was at least six feet high and topped with spikes. They were obviously prepared for unwelcome guests. I could hear the dogs barking in the distance. The taxi driver pushed the creaking gates open and we drove in.

Around the sprawling farmhouse, sugarcane grew thick and dense. At the sound of our horn, a young dark-skinned girl holding a child on her hip appeared at the door. The child was fairer than her. Both of them stared at me, two pairs of dark, suspicious eyes. The girl did not look more than twelve years old. But there was a tiredness about her, and she was dressed in a saree, not a frock. The child in her arms looked barely a year old. As she stood eyeing me warily, another child crawled out and stood up precariously, holding onto her clothes. Perhaps the girl was older than I imagined, if she already had two children.

I got out of the car and asked her in Hindi who she was.

'Shanti,' she replied with that typical Bhojpuri lilt, as the child in her arms fixed me with an unblinkingly serious stare.

'Are these your children?'

'Yes,' she nodded.

'Do you live here?'

She adjusted the child on her hip with expert ease. 'I live here and in the city. I work for sahib.'

'Santji?'

'Jitu.' It was a whisper. She sniffled and wiped her eyes with the edge of her saree. Certainly, she showed more emotion over Jitu than Binny had in her televised interview or her emails. I looked carefully at the children who, no doubt, had Atwal blood in them.

'Bechari. When did you come here to the farm?'

'They brought us three days ago.'

'Who else is with you?'

Before she could answer, another woman, much older than her, came out and started shouting at the younger girl to get inside. She stood aggressively in front of me and blocked my way to the house. She was obviously a figure of authority, dressed in a crisp white saree pinned neatly at the collar of her blouse. Her dark hair, shot through with grey, was pulled back, and she wore severe black-rimmed spectacles.

'What do you want?'

'I've come to look around the house because I am helping the police with the case.'

'No one sent us any information. I am afraid you will have to go.'

For a moment I was stumped by her bluntness.

'Look, why don't you call Amarjit and check with him? He asked me to come here and meet you.'

She hesitated slightly on hearing Amarjit's name. I was confident that she would not be able to get through immediately because he would be in meetings, and that would give me some breathing space to look around.

'I can give you his mobile phone number,' I added helpfully.

That convinced her that I was the genuine article. Mobile numbers of top bureaucrats are very precious commodities only given to the 'nears and dears'.

'All right,' she said grudgingly. 'I can't call Sir on his mobile but I'll try his office and see if there is some response. What is your name?'

'Simran Singh,' I said, trying to figure out how I could get into the house.

As we were talking I heard a steady pounding sound in the distance, as though someone was hammering a nail into a wall.

The woman in front of me seemed uncertain about what to do, but as the noise increased she told me I would have to stay in the veranda while she went in to make the phone call. I nodded and sat down on a chair, acquiescent and docile. As soon as she went in, I scurried to the last door at the end of the corridor and tried opening it. It was then that I heard her, very clearly. My heart stopped beating.

It was a fearsome sound. A steady rising crescendo of screams from inside the house.

I needed a witness. I beckoned to the driver.

'I'm going in,' I told him. He looked shaken at the sound. It was high pitched and almost like an animal in pain. 'You have to come with me.'

He still seemed worried. I wanted to slap him for his indecision but instead, gritted my teeth and said as quietly as I could, without showing any sign of panic, 'Someone in there may be hurt and I want to know what's going on. I may need your help.'

To his credit, he crept in after me. The house had high ceilings and was completely dark; the only light came from the ventilators above our heads.

It was surprisingly easy to find her. The door was open, and the woman I had met earlier was bent over the sprawled figure on the bed.

I knew her the moment I saw her.

The open hair, the sightless eyes gazing at the ceiling. The excruciatingly thin body, the face with the scar. Only, now she was clothed, not like in the photograph.

Not Durga, thank god, was my first thought.

She was chained to the bed, and her hands clenched and unclenched relentlessly as she screamed out unintelligible words that only she could understand. All the words, all the anger that she had suppressed for so many years poured out of her, over and over again, making no impression whatsoever on the world around her. Her head rolled from side to side, and her blank eyes opened and shut as she tried to articulate to some unseen person her anguish in an unending repetitive cycle. Her head thumped against the headboard as she pushed herself up. Froth poured from the corner of her mouth. The beautiful, once soft lips twisted back in an animal snarl as she shouted out her wrath and her helplessness.

I could not tell if it was the same room that I had seen in the photograph, but at least it appeared to be clean, and the woman, who was probably a nurse, was stroking her forehead and obviously trying to calm the girl down.

'Sharda.' I stepped into the room.

The woman tending to her whirled around, startled.

'Please leave the room,' she said, but without much conviction.

'Why have you chained her?'

'There is no other way for us to keep her in here. If we leave her free, she runs out and picks up little children and hides them. She locked up Shanti's son in a cupboard for one day, and he almost suffocated.'

'Is there a doctor who comes for her?'

'No.'

'So who gives you instructions on what to do?'

She hesitated. 'Manubhai and I manage now. Earlier the family would come, Jitu came. But now…'

I looked over her shoulder at Shanti, who was crouched on the floor while her baby suckled at her breast. Next to her sat another, equally young girl, also pregnant. Jitu had been productive.

'And these girls also help?'

'They try, but they are totally untrained.'

'Are you trained?'

For the first time a flicker of emotion crossed her face. 'I worked for thirty years in the police hospital.'

Not a terrific recommendation, but at least she would have some familiarity with medicine.

'And when did they hire you?'

'Just about a year ago. Before that she was kept in a terrible condition, like an animal. No clothes, dirty, lice in her hair. Now I make her bathe, and clean her at least twice a day.'

As she spoke to me, she kept stroking Sharda's forehead and the soothing touch must have helped, for the screaming stopped. Sharda was moaning quietly to herself now, and trying to sit up. She peered at me, but like a blind woman trying to see. Her clothes, just a long kaftan, had ridden up her legs, revealing scabs and scars from old wounds. Her hand, chained to the bed, fluttered weakly, twisting like a white butterfly. She was pale, paler than anyone I had ever seen; even her hair was white. She was only twenty years old, and the mother of a young son, but she looked like she was a frail woman of sixty. Her skin hung in emaciated strings from her bones. What a price to pay for one summer of love.

The nurse left the room to get some medicines and I turned to Shanti.

'Does Ramnath come here?'

She nodded.

'Does he pay your salary?'

She nodded again. And then I asked the question that mattered to me the most.

'And does Harpreetsir, the green-eyed man, also come to see her?'

She nodded once more. I now knew more than I wanted

to know but it was all part of this great and wonderful thing called life, wasn't it? You think you know it all, when suddenly, wham! something blows all your illusions away.

Had this poor girl been more careful about whom she loved, she would not have been so used and abused. For this one man she had lost everything, and all she got was a long chain to tie her down to a bed for the rest of her life. At least the one thing they were all clear about was that they needed to keep her alive. For a reason which, no doubt, I would discover soon enough.

I told the driver to come out with me, while I dialled Gurmit.

'I found Sharda.' I could not stop the trembling even as I said it.

I was suddenly shaking like a leaf, and tears were flowing down my face.

He said he would come immediately. He said he had more information about Durga. Some papers he had managed to get from the remand house warden, for a price, no doubt.

I sat on the veranda like a stone till he appeared. I had never been more relieved to see anyone in my life. He went inside and despite strong protests from the nurse, who finally withdrew mumbling into the other room to dial Amarjit's number, he took photographs of Sharda. She still lay on the bed, oblivious to the new presence and the camera lights shining in her eyes.

I sat outside, still unable to move. When Gurmit had completed his work, I asked him if we should take her away with us. But the nurse refused to unlock the handcuff. When Gurmit threatened her with all sorts of dire consequences, she said that the keys were with Ramnath.

While we were arguing, Manubhai, who had been away all this while, appeared, and I realized the game was up. He told us he was going to call Ramnath, and that ensured that we left immediately. He tried to snatch Gurmit's camera but Gurmit quickly put an arm around me and hustled me out to the car. I kept protesting and shouting, but what I said I still don't remember.

Most of that day still comes and goes in flashes of memory, a bit like when sudden lightning illuminates a dark and stormy night. But the rest of the time everything remains hidden, obscure, a meaningless jumble of shapes and voices.

In the car, I finally allowed myself to break down completely. I don't remember whose car it was or what I said to the driver I had come with. I put my head on Gurmit's shoulder and all the way to Amritsar, I cried. When he handed me the papers, the diary maintained by Durga in the remand home, I cried some more.

He gave me printouts of Binny's worried emails and a picture of the green-eyed child, Rahul, and the tiny doll-like Mandy. It was Rahul I could not help staring at, again and again. Why had I resisted the obvious for so long? There was an enormous sense of relief that at least I was now coming close to the truth, but there was also an aching sense of loss.

ॐ

To simransingh@hotmail.com

this is the 4th day i am writing to u but there is no response. I have tried the guesthouse, i finally got the number from amarjit's office but they say u've gone out for the day. i don't know what is happening, and i am hearing all sorts of rumours from various journalists. is it true that they have taken durga to amritsar. why why why?

Where are u, i am sick with worry. i got another call from harpreetsir but i told my mother to tell him i'm unwell. i really am—i thought u would be able to get durga out of it... u know as a child she was almost killed, like her sister by that family? they never wanted these girls. which is why she was so protective of me. she had suffered all of 14 years, imagine knowing you are an unwanted dispensable baby. she was only angry because of that. they are using her anger against her. don't let them.

please write back soon. love from all of us, binny

FOURTEEN

It started out as another strange day. The doctor came in and they removed all my clothes and even my kara and earrings, and put me in a hospital gown. They said they needed to run some tests on me and gave me an injection and so I went to sleep again. I don't know if I ate anything because everything seemed to become a blur of day and night. I was put in a van and taken to another place and here they were very strict. I could hear people screaming and shouting, and there were iron bars everywhere in the cell I was taken to. But I knew it wasn't a regular jail because everyone kept pushing me and saying, 'one more paagal has joined us'.

That's how I knew that they had finally brought me where once they had kept Didi. They gave me a pill to swallow but I haven't taken it as yet. I'll take it only after I finish this letter, so I can note down everything clearly.

I asked a nurse for some paper and a pencil so I could write to you. I know you will come for me. I know you won't forget me or hurt me. She has promised to post this for me. But now that I am officially crazy, who knows if she will actually do it.

Funny how it's become a habit. You were someone I didn't know till two weeks ago, and now I think of you every day, talk to you in my head, write you these letters all the time. Some day perhaps, if you ever find me, I'll tell you everything. Really. Everything.

I don't really blame Ramnath, you know. Ramnath was a loyal agent of my parents—he was only following their orders, even after their death. Somehow I was prepared for all this because I knew one way or the other the events of that night had to catch up with me. How could they let me go so easily, those ghosts from the past who had wanted to ensure my death right from the time of my birth? In these last three months, finally freed of all of them for a short time at least, I often wondered what life would have been like if I had been loved and wanted and cared for. If I had a mother who did not hate me because I was a girl.

It was a fantasy that Didi and I had sometimes indulged in when we played our secret games. She would be both my mother and my lover, because we had no one else who understood the meaning of love.

I am prepared now. I am prepared for the beatings and the electric shocks and the torture and I am prepared to lose my mind and become like Didi. I want you to know that I am not scared at all, rather, I welcome it.

Maye ni maye, main ik shikra yaar banaya… remember?

My madness will help Ramnath in his final attempt to take what he has envied us for so long. The Bhoot Bangla, emptied of all its annoying denizens. How long can a man plot and plan before he finally gets within his grasp his heart's desire? How clever he had been was clear to me but I will never know the full extent of how foolish I have been. Yet… honestly speaking, I am strangely happy and even relieved to go under, into the darkness. It will be good to finally escape permanently into the other world where I will not remember anything of that dreadful night or the horrible life which went before.

Having lived with all these terrible memories, it will be wonderful to finally lose control over this clever, logical mind that plots and plans and worries, always thinking thinking thinking...

All right, I made all those promises for Didi and for Binny and him. I swore I would be quiet and let them take over, so long as Didi and I were together. In here I am finally liberated to say everything. In here, even if I tell anyone anything, who will believe me? And does it matter, because I wasn't supposed to be here anyway.

Didi and I seem to have a joint destiny. We were saved from death at birth to be forced into a kind of living hell. My only hope now is that Ramnath keeps his promise that they will eventually lock me up with my sister and in our madness, at least, we will be together again. My sister, my mother, my lover.

Hopefully, the darkness will come very quickly.

We drove at breakneck speed to Amritsar. Somehow we were convinced that we had to reach her soon, because no doubt Ramnath would need evidence of Durga's madness. And how else could this be done, unless he got his friends to induce it? To manufacture the reports, to inject the medicines. To deliver the electric shocks that were forbidden—possibly once again given to her, like they did with Sharda, without anaesthesia.

I hoped that the director would be able to resist these demands. The truth was, of course, that the boss was sometimes the last to find out what had actually happened. Greased palms often did the trick lower down in the rungs.

The familiar red and grey building flew out at me like a vulture. I knew I was talking too much, walking too fast, behaving as though I were a lunatic myself. I almost dragged Gurmit with me to the reception. *Hurry, hurry, hurry,* a voice in my head kept whispering. *It may be too late, too late, too late.* Sharda's broken voice rang in my ears, her hands clawing the air, her agonized face contorting over and over again in the remembered rituals of pain and degradation. The nonsensical language she spoke was laden with grief. She had forgotten all the words familiar to us because none of those words could tell us what she had been through.

So much had been cleared up in the journey to Amritsar as we went through Durga's dairies, though I wished I could have read them in less tragic circumstances.

In many ways this was the story Gurmit had wanted to publish even before the murders, especially about the female foeticide. He had found out about it from the local clinics to which Santji had donated large amounts of money, and where the doctors were far too obliged to him to register a case with the police. He even owned a clinic where abortions were routinely carried out. But, of course, the newspaper editors had rejected the claims, especially of Ramnath's involvement, because after all, the man was the father of two daughters and was an outstanding, highly decorated police officer.

But Gurmit had found out other troubling facts which he did not quite understand at the time. He had discovered that Harpreetsir, that unfairly beautiful man, had been meeting Durga sometimes at home, sometimes elsewhere, in small hotels on the outskirts of Jullundur. Ma Sukhi was correct as always. Twice the tutor had driven out of town with her, but Gurmit had not imagined that there could be a larger plot or that perhaps Harpreetsir had a larger lesson to teach Durga. Something that would annihilate her entire existence and along with it, all the people she had ever known.

Still searching for the love she had lost when her sister disappeared, Durga had perhaps been persuaded to turn to Harpreetsir. In him she had found someone who loved her sister. And through him and his body she could love her sister once more. In her desperation she had never understood that he was using her emotions and her sexuality to manipulate her.

Initially, perhaps, he found it flattering, but ultimately he used the child to take his revenge, and perhaps for something more. He stoked her anger and her hurt at their disregard and the ghastly misuse of their daughters. Like a good teacher, in their secret meetings he taught her the meaning of rebellion. He explained to her, over afternoons of lovemaking perhaps, who her real enemies were. He helped her formulate, this young wounded creature who had lost her anchor in life, the plan that would save Binny's child and avenge the cruelties inflicted on Sharda. I had known how intelligent and seductive he could be at my first meeting—how much more difficult would it have been for a young girl to resist him? In the meantime, he was careful to build up his own reputation as the perfect, caring, idealistic man.

After all, once he lost Sharda, he even married a woman who had been burnt by her former in-laws for bringing insufficient dowry, and adopted her young daughter. We had learnt this from him, and believed it all. The outer image was infallible.

What he had not told us, and what we had now found out, was how he had encouraged Durga in her blind adulation. But it was all done in a subtle way and the tipping point probably came for her when the family decided to abort Binny's baby. Was he the man who helped plan that macabre night? They say that drugs are often used to brainwash murderers, but here it was love, wasn't it? The same love that had destroyed one sister was now being used against the other.

The helpless child who pined for affection fell into the trap as she was twisted and turned like a plastic doll and bent into shape by the gentle lover. Innocent and naïve and convinced that he had a plan for her, a new life promised to her, she was pliable and obedient.

Perhaps he helped her buy the poison and suggested to Durga that Binny take his own son, Rahul, out of the country. He may even have been present in the house that night to orchestrate the proceedings, to make sure the fear was dissolved and the plan well executed. He probably used his own power over her to convince her to stay on, so that there was an obvious culprit. From her diary, it appeared that he had raped her. He knew she was loyal to the last breath and would never betray him. She had kept her promise.

Gurmit had another theory too. Since Ramnath knew all along where Sharda was, Durga was probably told that Sharda would be looked after in the future, if she followed their instructions. This was the other part of the bargain. After the deaths, the final reconciliation.

Durga might have sent the photographs of her sister to the press in the futile hope that the truth would be discovered, and her family's secrets revealed before the apocalypse. But nothing happened. In one last attempt, she had even asked me for the books at home because she wanted me to find Sharda's photograph and look for her. But I had not understood.

Harpreetsir showed Durga how Sharda had been kept, in filth and dirt. Then she was cleaned up, and the police nurse was brought in. For the grateful child who could not help her sister in any other way, it was enough instigation to do whatever she was asked to. All the years of exclusion and repression had programmed her to respond.

It was a dangerous combination and one that Harpreetsir enjoyed using. He pushed and pushed at her until she reached the point of complete submission to his demands. The night of the murders as recorded in her diaries demonstrated the power he had over her.

But what next? We had no proof of anything, and yet here we were, trying to get a young girl out of a lunatic asylum as though it were the easiest thing in the world. At the entrance, I took a deep breath and turned to Gurmit.

'Listen, before we go in, no matter what happens, let me just say I really like you and thanks a lot. I was angry with you earlier, said a lot of things, I know—but you were doing your job, just as I am doing mine now. This sounds like a foolishly heroic statement, so I hesitate to say it, but if we can save her somehow...'

'I like you too,' interrupted Gurmit, not looking fifteen years younger than me any more, but much older suddenly. His expression made me wonder what he was really thinking.

Why have I got involved with this mad forty-five-year-old social worker? Or perhaps, I could be arrested any moment if I do anything more to antagonize Ramnath.

'You know, I have so many so-called friends in Jullundur, people I have known since the day I was born, practically. So I have no idea why, instead of all of them, I trust you, a young sardar I met barely three days ago.'

'One week. I sent you flowers, remember? There must be some mystical connection between us.'

'Is that a promise?'

He smiled. And I liked the way his smile went all the way up to his eyes. Together we marched into the director's office and asked to meet Prakash Goel. The receptionist remembered me, but was reluctant to let us in, saying, 'Sir is in a meeting with the SP, Mister Ramnath.'

She did not know it was like a red rag to a bull.

Gurmit flashed his media card and I argued that it was urgent. Before she could stop us, we were both inside the room facing three very surprised people who were, until that moment, calmly drinking tea. Prakash appeared the most astonished of the three.

Harpreetsir smiled politely, his eyes exuding their familiar warmth. Ramnath gave a mock salute and exclaimed, 'Hullo, hullo, hullo.' There was no anxiety that I could discern on either face. Suddenly I began to feel a little foolish. I kept Sharda's image firmly in my mind so that I could hang on to my anger.

'Simran, would you care to wait while I finish with these gentlemen?' Prakash asked.

'We are actually here to meet all three of you,' I said and sat down firmly on a chair.

It's a funny thing. You can be fairly certain you're right when you are thinking up a theory, but when you are face to face with the persons concerned, theories begin to drop down like pigeon shit on your head. These were such regular, normal guys. Okay, one was a sharp dresser and the other was a far-too-good-looking tutor but was that enough reason to hang them? I had no concrete evidence, only hearsay, Durga's diaries, and Gurmit's investigation. Gurmit probably had the same thought as he raised his eyebrows at me. But we knew that we could not be weak at this point. Our theories were all we had… that, and our visit to Sharda.

The main thing was not to get too flustered and somehow get Durga out.

'You turn up in the oddest places,' said Ramnath. 'Amrinder did warn me.' He laughed and adjusted the crease of his trousers as he leaned back and crossed his legs. His polished black shoes gleamed like car headlights, just as I remembered them.

What was it about this man that was so annoying, apart from his wife and mother-in-law? I could think of at least a hundred things, but now was not the time to list them.

Harpreetsir did not laugh, but fixed me with a sorrowful look. Gurmit gave his visiting card to Prakash and glanced quizzically at Ramnath.

'I thought you said in your interview that Durga was not going to be moved here?'

'She probably has schizophrenia, like her sister.'

'Which you discovered just three days ago?'

'Can I see the psychiatrist's report on the basis of which you shifted her? I met her just three days ago too, she was fine. Absolutely normal. Just depressed and very quiet, as she has been since I first saw her,' I added quickly.

My phone rang. Mother.

'I've just got another response to the advertisement. You'll be so thrilled,' she trilled joyfully.

'Mother, I'll call you back.' I could not help sounding annoyed. My mother knew the perfect place to discuss matrimonial alliances: in a lunatic asylum.

I switched the phone off, staring straight at Ramnath, who was smirking at me. In a peculiar way, my mother's random phone call unleashed a cold anger inside me. I felt my hatred for this man crush every last doubt.

'I don't think you moved her because of any suspected bouts of mental illness. I think you moved her because of Sharda's photograph. I gave it to her. You got worried that someone knew about her and would force a confession out of Durga, which would implicate the two of you.'

Even as I spoke, I realized I sounded horribly glib. It was all conjecture, after all.

Harpreetsir remained expressionless. He was careful not to look at Ramnath. Ramnath gave a deep sigh and appeared tired and exasperated, but willing to humour me. He spoke slowly, as though to a dumb child.

'I don't know what photograph you're talking about. Right now, we need a proper medical report on Durga. Simran, with all due respect, we cannot depend on, excuse me as I say it, your rather amateurish attempt at psychoanalysis. She has conducted a serious crime and must—'

'You should be very careful what you say next,' Gurmit cut in abruptly. 'You are showing extreme prejudice towards a young woman and there are three witnesses to it...' I looked at him, astonished. I had not heard such authority or aggression in his voice before.

Ramnath was stumped, perhaps reading future not-socomplimentary headlines in Gurmit's tone. But his confusion lasted for only a minute. He continued suavely, 'I think you still don't know the facts of the case. Let me explain these to you, and also to Prakash, because he is new here and must be very surprised at the way we are conducting ourselves.'

'I have enough photographs and interviews to know the facts. I have been working on this for nearly a year, especially since I got Sharda's photograph. The last time, you managed to get the publication stopped. But this time I am giving the material to a TV channel, which is going to run the story of how a young girl was driven insane by a police officer just because she fell in love with the wrong person. That she was raped and tortured within the asylum, that her tutor whom she loved then began to abuse her sister, and that now the sister is also in the asylum. We have Durga's diaries right here with us. They will be telecast live on the news channel tonight. Suddenly, *you* are going to be the story.'

I could see Prakash was becoming distinctly uncomfortable. He wiped his forehead and looked helplessly at all of us. He was hearing far too much, and looked like he wasn't sure he wanted to be involved in any of it.

I leaned forward and told him gently, 'I don't think you have the jurisdiction to keep an innocent and sane young girl in this place. It will be terrible if the TV cameras arrive here; they are difficult to get out once they sniff out a story. Remember that case at Central Hospital? They stuck around outside for almost a month, and I think at the end of it the hospital got into trouble, so many doctors were sacked...

'On the other hand, if you allow Durga to go back with us... and if the police withdraw the case on the basis that there is no evidence... there would be no scandal.'

Gurmit nodded. 'I am willing to withdraw the story from the TV channel, if you agree.'

There was a long silence. Then the director finally spoke up.

'Ramnathji... I am sorry, I think Simran is correct. I feel I may have the wrong information on this girl and I would be very hesitant to do anything that would harm her.'

Harpreetsir spoke up for the first time since we had entered the room. 'We don't want to harm her, either. You and Simranji have the wrong impression.'

The ever persuasive dulcet tones, the hurt in those green eyes. Even now, knowing what I knew, I could feel the ground slip beneath my feet. It was so easy to think that I was wrong and he was correct.

'Harpreetji...' I decided to be as formal as he was. 'I am sure you too have her best interests at heart. After all, your son is her nephew and this is going to be a long association. I also know from her diaries that you were rather... fond of her. The sister was just sixteen years old when she bore your child, and Durga is only fourteen. I am sure Ramnathji will agree with us that this could be considered rape if we wanted to press charges.'

A pained expression crossed Harpreetsir's face. How could I use this terrible four-letter word for him? After all, he had only been trying to befriend two young girls who were ill-treated by their own family.

'I am really sorry you have such a poor opinion of me. I came here to help Durga recover, not for any other reason. You cannot imagine how much Sharda means to me.'

From his expression, I realized why it was important to keep Sharda alive. The proof that she was Rahul's mother lay in her DNA, probably the only part of her that was still functioning with normal efficiency. Gurmit had done his research well. All the material his paper had not allowed him to publish was spilling out now.

'Ramnathji... our deal is very simple. Please let Durga come home with us, and let us see if we can work out a compromise over the house.' That was what he really wanted, wasn't it?

For the first time, a reluctant relief flashed in Ramnath's eyes. The Company Bagh house whose every chandelier he had counted in his dreams might not slip away after all. Perhaps he could still share the spoils with Harpreet.

'What is the guarantee that you will stick to your word?' The question slipped out of his smooth-tongued mouth.

At this oblique admission that what we had said was correct, Prakash abruptly got up and stopped following our conversation in half-embarrassed horror. Like me, he was still absorbing the reality of life in the wild west. It certainly wasn't pleasant. He had invited these gentlemen in to discuss a possible schizophrenic case and instead, was being dragged into a conversation about rape and murder and property disputes. Since Prakash belonged to a family of straightforward medical doctors who had lived and practiced abroad for fifty years, he had completely forgotten the negotiations of a normal Indian life in which people's destinies are routinely bartered.

'I think I'm going to make arrangements for the child to leave with you, Simran, in any case. If they want a police escort they can send one, but I don't think I can keep her.'

Harpreetsir turned to Ramnath. 'But you've given interviews saying the case has been solved?'

There was a sudden silence.

'Just tell the truth. Say you were given false information about Durga's involvement and that you are still looking for the culprit. That the doctors have certified she isn't insane.' Gurmit was resolute.

Ramnath spoke up. 'But all the evidence points to her.'

'We can also produce evidence that points to the two of you.'

It didn't take long for us to fine-tune the deal. Gurmit was to surrender his camera and Durga's diary in return for them letting her go. The sweetest moment came when a groggy and half-asleep Durga met us at the entrance. The next day we would go back and pick up Sharda, since special arrangements for her care would have to be made. At that time the rest of the papers would be handed over.

As we left the mental hospital, I could see Harpreetsir trying to find the words to tell me how wrongly I had judged him. How incorrect was my assessment and how much he had genuinely cared for the two girls. So much lay beneath the surface, so much hidden depth, but there was no real substance, only his own careful self-preservation and a constant yearning. For what? For acknowledgement, for admiration? 'Don't misunderstand me,' he said over and over again. I could not hide my repugnance but at the same time I was mesmerized by the wounded look in those hypnotic eyes. Could I have got him wrong after all?

As I carefully guided Durga to the car, she hesitated, even in her drug-induced state, when she passed by him. She held out a hand. 'Please don't leave me, don't leave.' There was a begging note in her voice that made me cringe. I brushed his hand aside and put her in the car, slamming the door in his woebegone face.

'Don't even try to contact her again,' I said. 'Or Sharda.'

'You still don't understand, do you?' He was still as soft-spoken as before. He seemed overcome with grief. 'I only wanted to help them. I love Sharda.'

I don't know why those words stuck with me, but I thought about them all the way back. In a way he was correct. The girls could never have avenged the death of their childhood on their own. They were far too innocent. He had helped them do that, but at a terrible price.

To <u>simransingh@hotmail.com</u>

Dear Simi, what a relief. I just saw a news flash that my angel has been released and is cleared of all charges. That is wonderful news... Gurmit called and said u were sleeping, and so was Durga and that you will both speak to me tomorrow. I cannot wait to hear from u. I am still feeling very unwell after the tension of the last few days. But call soon. With love Binny

FIFTEEN

12/04/08

They say nothing in life is easy and that we all have to struggle to find ourselves, and happiness. I suppose where I am now is finally a happy place. I have spent the last six months just resting and trying to become 'normal', trying to do what girls are supposed to do, wear pretty clothes and paint my nails and put on jewellery. But somehow, my mind keeps going back to that night and what actually happened. Of course I remember it, though you are constantly telling me that I must treat it like a nightmare, that I was forced to do certain things, that I did them primarily because I had been so unwanted and so unloved, that I did them for my sister, that I did them for Harpreetsir. And that I should not think about it any more and I must start this new life... I must forgive myself and learn to love myself, you say.

But how does one forget the tyranny of dreams? They have dominated my life from the start, their larger-than-life colours, their landscapes which breathe of a joyousness I can never have. I look at my poor sister, she did not escape the tyranny either. Why did she believe that dreams come true? Now she lives, not in a dream world, but in a world where her

nightmares are played out over and over again. I remember
her soft breasts and growing belly, her sweet smell as I
snuggled down with her, our night life of secret games...

I see her as she is, white haired and broken, eyes glazed with
drugs and fingers perpetually seeking, fluttering like birds,
seeking me, I know. She is reassured if I sit with her. She
stops moaning and using words I cannot understand and
instead strokes my face silently... In her I see all the sisters
and all the girls that my family has lost and buried, in her
I see the brown field behind the house where the babies were
suffocated. I cannot forget any of it, I cannot forget these
unfair dreams that force me to do different things... I want
to be like everyone else but the dreams don't let me rest, they
make me want and want and want...

They make me want to destroy the world and create it again,
make it more loving, make it more just... and then the anger,
the awful anger comes back and I really do feel like Durga,
the goddess Durga you showed me, with the myriad hands
and the skulls around her neck, the Durga who wants to
slash and tear and hurt and wound... in exactly the same
way in which those poor little babies were wounded. I don't
know when this rage will leave me... I know, when I go
back to school and start making friends, perhaps some of this
will recede. You tell me that right now I am still being swept
by the waves of an angry tide, but I must allow the sea to
grow calmer, and in the water I will find beautiful fish and
colourful plants and coral reefs, and I must learn to swim
with the tide, not fight it.

Binny will soon be here and perhaps the baby will distract me.
It will be lovely to see a normal baby girl, a healthy, much

*loved baby girl. I look forward to meeting Rahul, too, though
he may not come because of the adoption case.*

*And as for me? What will happen to me, the child who
should not have been born? I have not told you, but he sent
me an email yesterday. What does he want from me now,
will the past never leave me? At times his soft voice still echoes
in my ears, his hands on my body making me do things I
never wanted to do, making me learn things I never wanted
to know. He possessed me so completely after Didi left that I
used to think of him day and night. The truth is that he could
get inside my head and I have to admit, I never did anything
I did not want to. I know you say I was very young but I
wanted it all, I wanted him and, yes, I think I even wanted
them all dead. Will I ever be able to tell you that? Will you
listen?*

*While waiting for Didi to come back, I also thought, at the
end of the long dark tunnel he will come and rescue me,
and so I waited and waited and waited. Instead of him, you
came, and I know you will never tell me what he was doing
there that evening at the hospital. Even through the drugs I
remember seeing him, but somehow you always change the
subject. I think I can guess why.*

*So I don't know if I should reply to him. Will it upset you? I
dare not ask.*

Ultimately, this case, which I thought would be my last,
changed my life, didn't it? I came home with Durga. For

some reason I still don't know, Amarjit agreed when Ramnath suggested that Durga stay with me. I think the fact that he had sunk so low in my eyes may have finally hit home. He wanted all of us to start afresh, and perhaps he had always wanted to save Durga, just as he had told me. Since the police case was officially closed, my mother suddenly got a fourteen-year-old granddaughter, one with a rather colourful past. Funnily enough, they seemed to like each other. Perhaps my mother's frivolous lifestyle is a relief for Durga, after the intense depression she must have been under since her sister disappeared. All she needs is to feel loved and be secure. Already, she is sleeping better, and the dark circles under her eyes are getting fainter every day.

My mother enjoys cooking for her and they both spend hours in the kitchen, discussing recipes and trying out new ones. Everyone enjoys a second chance in life. Perhaps in this emotionally battered young girl my mother sees a chance to try and understand her own daughter. We have lived through enormous uncertainties and so we now try to make the house as cheerful as we can for Durga. We know how close we were to losing her forever. And in her eyes sometimes, I can see that she knows it too.

I have to say I decided that I did not want to know what happened that night, nine months ago, at the Company Bagh house. Somehow we had to bring closure to it and I thought that one day, when Durga could face up to her role on that horrible night and when she was sufficiently distanced from it all, she would tell me. The fact that she refuses to talk about her family very much, apart from sudden bursts of anger, makes me realize that she has not forgiven them either. Their patriarchal lifestyle, the way they treated their daughters, the suppression of their sexuality... I could write a whole textbook about the Atwal family. She often remembers with crystal clarity the burial grounds at the back, the stories of girl children routinely murdered, the inability of the two girls to even step out of the house. She still has not accepted this inhuman divide. What was wrong with her? The question continues to trouble her.

But of that night, except for the extracts in her diary, I know very little. She too appears to have forgotten it all. How had it happened? Was I worried that it might happen again, that she could be persuaded to turn against us? I doubt it. My own view is that she had been unloved and very lonely when Harpreetsir began his exploitation of her emotions. Now things are different. It is a relief to know that her relationship with him is behind her now. In time the childish tattoo on her arm will also fade.

The other reason why I refuse to know anything more about the murders is that we have worked out a compromise with Ramnath who is buying out the Company Bagh house at a price cheaper than the market rate. I don't think either Binny or Durga will be able to live there, so it is best to let it go. When Binny comes down they will sign the papers, and I will tell her everything. So far she doesn't know all the details of what happened because she is still very fragile and we must look after her. The shock of Durga being put in the mental hospital is something she still has not been able to come to terms with. She blames herself for it.

I know it's odd how I can still deal with everyone in this case though I have seen and know the worst side of them. I suppose all those years of working with jailbirds have toughened me up. The only thing that still moves me is

Durga, and the hope that I will be able to pull her out of this.

It's something I have always fought for, and wanted to do, to take a child out of jail into a free world and then help her, perhaps, to find a new life. My hope for redemption, will it finally happen?

Is this an experiment then? Am I trying to play god? Perhaps. Will I succeed? Who knows? It will all be worthwhile the day Durga becomes an independent working woman, with a family perhaps, and with someone who loves her.

So, of course, the real reason why I don't want to know about that night is that I have begun to care deeply for Durga. She needs a lifetime of love and protection. I am waiting for that moment when she somehow pulls out of the dark world into which she had been pushed and manages to break free. Free of those ghosts who haunted her and free of Harpreetsir, too. I still see those images in her eyes. She tells me how her sister had wanted to become a stockbroker, and how she herself dreams of being a doctor or an engineer. If she can put her mind to it, I am sure she can achieve anything, and that will be the real vindication of all her years of suffering. That will be the vindication of her sister's belief that they would manage to survive all the attempts to kill them. It will give a purpose to her life.

Sharda is going for therapy every day and the doctors think that with medication she will become calmer. She is already trying to communicate with Durga, who is the only one who seems to be able to get through to her.

My mother is uncomfortable sharing the house with this strange creature who speaks a peculiar language and is unable to look after herself. But I think she also feels sorry for her.

Fortunately, my father left us an enormous bungalow in South Delhi so if ever one doesn't want to meet the other, the upstairs/downstairs divide takes care of it. Dad's money is also providing a full-time nurse for Sharda. I don't think he would have objected.

As for me, my mother has almost given up on finding me a bridegroom. I think she has a sneaking liking for Gurmit, though, because she has not once complained about how he is too young for me. She flirts with him once in a while, and doesn't mind if he teases her and takes her out for coffee. He comes over for the weekends and we spend our time drinking beer and talking. Sometimes, thankfully, we do much more than that. For all the differences between us, we fit well together.

To <u>simransingh@hotmail.com</u>

Dear Simi, The oddest thing happened today. Harpreetsir showed up! Why didn't anyone tell me he is so gorgeous? And what lovely green eyes, u can drown in them. He looks a lot like Rahul, or is it the other way round, so now I understand why he wanted to meet us. And I am feeling better already. Mandy really liked him, too. So we're going out today and I'm taking him sightseeing. Wish me luck, Binny.

AUTHOR'S NOTE

While the characters and places in this book are entirely fictional, the events which take place are not. There is a complicity of corruption between the police, the judicial system, politicians, media and uncivil society. My father, Padam Rosha, is possibly one of the very few incorruptible police officers who was posted in northern India. He had the courage to stand up against powerful politicians—and he often paid the price for it. But as the case of Ruchika Girhotra has proved yet again, officers like him are few and far between, and gender issues are still treated with contempt.

ACKNOWLEDGEMENTS

It always helps a first-time novelist if people believe in her. I want to gratefully acknowledge my wonderful editor, Karthika V.K., for all her support and editorial inputs. To others at HarperCollins, particularly Neelini Sarkar, Pradipta Sarkar and Shantanu Ray Chaudhuri, I extend a heartfelt thanks. A million shukriyas are owed to Meghnad, my husband, and Mallika, my daughter, for their clear and unbiased opinions, and to my parents, Padam and Rajini Rosha, and Gaurav, my son, for their valuable inputs towards the book and understanding of what is often a chaotic life.

I also owe a huge debt to Khushwant Singh (though this was not the book he wanted me to write first). It was his belief that I could write that made it possible for me to imagine I could.

I am also grateful to Julian Friedman, my agent, and Simon Petherick, my UK publisher, for the idea that Simran, the central character in the book, should reappear in a continuing book series. So watch out for the return of Simran!